The Regan McHenry Real Estate Mysteries

The Death Contingency
Backyard Bones
Buying Murder
The Widow's Walk League
The Murder House
A Neighborly Killing
The Two-Faced Triplex

Other books by Nancy Lynn Jarvis

Mags and the AARP Gang

Cozy Food: 128 Cozy Mystery Writers Share Their Favorite Recipes

The Murder House

A Regan McHenry Real Estate Mystery

Nancy Lynn Jarvis

Good Read Mysteries
An Imprint of Good Read Publishers

**Good Read
Mysteries**

Good Read Mysteries © is a registered trademark of Good Read Publishers
301 Azalea Lane, Santa Cruz, California 95060

Copyright © 2013 by Nancy Kille

Library of Congress Control Number: 2013955280

ISBN: 978-0-9835891-5-0

Printed in the United States of America

www.GoodReadMysteries.com

Books are available at special quantity discounts through the website.

To all the people who, like me, love to tell their favorite ghost stories over dinner.

And, here's mine:

When I was in high school, I befriended a girl whose family had recently moved to our area and purchased a hundred-year-old house. She told me she discovered there was a ghost in her closet. She said her ghost, whom she now considered a friend, told her what her name was and that she had died in the house. My friend's ghost told her the year and cause of her death, as well.

My high school friend shared her sighting with her parents who immediately worried that their daughter was not adjusting well to the move. They feared she was creating imaginary friends, fine for a four-year-old child, but unacceptable for a sixteen-year-old. They set out to disprove her ghost by researching their house's history.

It took some time and effort, but you know what the results of their research were, don't you? That's right: all the details my friend's ghost told her were true.

Acknowledgements

A proper acknowledgement always starts with my husband Craig, without whom I couldn't do this. He reads, does the initial editing when the books are a mess, finds flaws in reasoning, asks why, figures out my computer and the website — even tastes cookies — to make the books work.

Once again, special thanks go to Editor Morgan Rankin for her many skills.

The Murder House

House

Nancy Lynn Jarvis

Every real estate agent has a ghost story or two to tell.

Most are explained away easily enough. The something that was seen out of the corner of his eye by a Realtor sitting alone in a vacant house might have been the indoor shadow cast by a bird flying by.

The unearthly sound heard outside could have been made by an unseen fox or frog.

Houses creaking and groaning? That's caused by the normal expansion and contraction of house members as homes heat up and cool down in the course of the day.

But my ghost story isn't as easy to dismiss because it involves the Murder House, a dwelling with a past and a reputation. An unsolved double murder took place inside and neighbors say they've seen ghosts in the house at night.

Regan McHenry

1

It was a pleasing house, cozy rather than spacious, like something Thomas Kincade might have imagined for one of his paintings. The board and batten siding was painted a creamy color as comforting as a glass of warm milk. The window sashes were done in humble cranberry and the front door was a deep forest green set off by a polished brass kick-plate and equally bright handle trim that glinted in the afternoon sun.

Redwood trees towered behind the house and at its sides, stately green and brown sentinels, but the house was south facing so they didn't cast a pall of shadows over it like they would have on a less perfectly situated dwelling. Trees had probably grown in front of the house at some point, too, given the nature of forests; if any had though, they had been removed.

Broad brick steps interspersed with pocket-sized patios that jutted into the manicured proximate gardens cascaded from the elevated house to the rich green lawns and guest parking below.

Regan climbed out of her car and took in the house and its surroundings.

"You're picture perfect, aren't you?" She spoke to the house as if it were an animate being. "You're supposed to be a derelict with a cruel past, but you look comfortable and charming. When did that happen? When did you, the most notorious house in Bonny Doon, take up such welcoming and benign airs?"

She ducked back into her car, grabbed her briefcase, and started up the steps. She had done her research for the meeting — she liked being prepared — but had already decided her visit was as much about getting a read on the house and its owner as it was about getting the listing. If her instincts told her there was anything untoward about either of them, she'd take a pass.

She remembered walking into a house in Aptos once where the hair on the back of her neck stood up the moment she crossed the threshold. She had turned on her heel and fled — she couldn't even preview the house, let alone show it to buyers — because there was something palpably cold and menacing that she sensed immediately. She planned to leave this house just as quickly if she picked up a similarly bad vibe.

Regan rang the doorbell and took a step backward, facing the door while she waited for the owner to open it, unwilling to turn her back on the house to enjoy the gardens like she would have done at any other property.

A brutal double murder had taken place inside the house almost two decades earlier and the killer had never been caught. One of the victims was a real estate broker, Roger Commons, a man she had met when she was in her early twenties and brand new to the business, who got by more on his charisma and good looks than his negotiating skills. The other victim was one of the house's owners, a female client of his.

The coroner had determined both had died at the same time or at least so close together in time that it was impossible to determine who died first. The female owner's throat had been slit, the realtor had been bludgeoned to death; but from the location of the bodies, the blood spatter in the bedroom where the owner's body was found, and the gore that corresponded with the broker's body in the entry foyer, it was clear they had not died together.

There were rumors the house was haunted. Regan had often overheard tales told at the unpancake breakfasts, fundraisers for the local volunteer firefighters, but never at the fundraiser dinners and dances that happened at night. Locals, it seemed, were willing to talk about the house during daylight hours, but reluctant to do so after dark.

At a recent event, one neighbor whispered she had heard wailing coming from the house, especially on dark nights, and had seen a dark-haired woman in a red dress materialize in an upstairs window. The neighbor said the figure called for help and then raised her arm and cowered at some unseen terror before vanishing as suddenly as she had appeared. Other neighbors oohed and nodded and added their own tales of sightings, undeterred by the conundrum of how one could perceive hair color or dress color in the dark. Several also agreed they had seen a moving bluish ball of light; and some said they had recently seen the light assume a human form as it slipped through the trees by the house.

Murder always generated gossip and speculation. The murders in this house caused more talk than usual because officially they remained unsolved.

Long-time realtors were particularly aware of the house's history because one of their own died there, and to Santa Cruz realtors who remembered what happened, like Regan did, the house was known as the Murder House.

With all the memories and imaginings going through her mind, Regan jumped involuntarily when the front door opened with a shrill squeal.

"Yes, I know. You don't have to tell me. I have to do something to stop that squeaking."

"Definitely," Regan smiled her greeting to the man opening the door.

"Remind me again, please, which one are you? I've had so many real estate agents come through, I've lost my place," the slightly built man said somberly. A broad smile erupted on his face and he laughed out loud, "I'm kidding, I'm kidding, well, sort of, at least. Come on in, won't you? Should I call you Regan or Mrs. McHenry?"

"I'm Regan," she tried to sound let down, "and not your first choice or interview? How disappointing," she teased as they shook hands.

"True. But you'll forgive me that, as long as you're my last," he laughed again, "won't you?"

She liked him immediately. Both he and his house felt amiable and engaging. The way he tried to get a rise out of her reminded her of how her oldest son, Ben, tried to shock her when he was a teenager; but instead of unsettling her, the way the young man spoke made her feel like they were sharing a joke. She was at ease with him, and even though she wasn't old enough to be his mother, she felt like he was one her boys.

"I should warn you right up front, though, if you're like your predecessors and tell me the only way to sell my house is to give it away, I will try again.

"I've learned you realtors seem to favor sitting at kitchen tables to talk. Follow me." He stepped back to let her come farther inside and then led the way through the living room and dining room into a kitchen-decorating-magazine's concept of perfection. The counters were granite, the appliances stainless steel, and the cupboards cherry and definitely custom. He motioned her toward a chair, inviting her to take a seat in surroundings that were not only clearly expensive but, she surmised, were recently redone because they showed no tell-tale signs of even minor wear.

"I can't play the innocent game with you, can I Regan? You've probably been in the real estate sales game long enough to have heard of my house and its past. I won't get anywhere waiting for you to give me a value and pretending I forgot to mention two murders were committed here, will I?"

"No you can't, and no you won't. In fact, if you tried that maneuver with me, I'd already be on my way out the front door." She smiled as she spoke, but knowingly, and her words were delivered with a certainty he couldn't miss. "Shall I call you Josh?"

He nodded his head yes. "It's been more than three years since anyone died here. After filling out papers with several new agents — agents who didn't dismiss me outright because they didn't know about the house's past until they were warned by more experienced agents — I know the three-year limit is all the disclosure that's legally required. Why do I have to let people know about the murders since it's been nineteen years since they happened?"

"You've already answered your own question: the house's reputation is out there. Your house is notorious, and for your own protection, you need to let the less well informed know about the property before they buy it, or you'll risk litigation when they find out afterwards."

He sighed and looked away like a beaten dog. "My uncle gave me the house free and clear when I graduated from college. After sitting empty in the woods since ... for so many years, it was habitable but a wreck. I planned to live here and work on the house as I could afford to.

"Unfortunately one day I went to one of those seminars about flipping houses and got all excited. I thought if I really tripped it out, I could sell it for enough profit to buy a little condo by the beach, which is where I want to be, and still have enough left over to pay off my student loans.

"I had no idea how expensive it would be to get my house to what it looks like now. It needed everything; I had to borrow a lot more money to fix it up than I intended and I used credit cards to do it, which was a bad idea. Now that it looks perfect, I'm in hock up to my eyeballs, my condo and debt payoff dreams are over, and you realtors are telling me I can't even sell this house for as much money as I put into it. It's just not fair."

"It is what it is. Let's see if we can figure out how to work with what we have."

"Are you going to wish me well and leave like all the other experienced agents when I tell you the ballpark number I need to get for this house is more than $300,000?"

"You've got ten minutes to convince me not to," she played his take-aback game. "You have to answer my questions truthfully, no half-truths allowed, even if you don't like telling me what I want to know. And you have to tell me why you want to sell. Then I'll be completely candid with you about the value of your house and my marketing plans for it, and we can decide if we can work together or if you should move on to the next name on your list."

"Deal."

"First, you said you own the house outright. You didn't put a mortgage on it to finance your improvements?"

"That's right."

"And you said your uncle gave you the house. Is he on title?"

"No. I think he should have been, though. My parents owned the house, but it wasn't paid for when my mother died. My father hasn't been seen since my mom ... most people think he killed her and that realtor ... and that after, he ran off.

"My uncle was close to our family; he was executor of the estate and my godfather. He took me in and has been like a father to me ever since. I didn't know he was doing it, but he kept paying the mortgage until he paid it off, and he got my father off the title — had him declared dead or something after so many years — so I became the sole owner.

"He could have told me to sell it and pay him back for all

those years of house payments and taxes — I think that would have been fair — but Uncle Jake is a great guy; he turned the house over to me. He said I should live here, be happy here, and keep the house in the family. He said that was the best way to handle the past: to not let it win.

"So that's what I did, at least the first part of it, until that seminar. Since then it's been a struggle to keep up with all I owe; I'm getting tired of trying so hard."

"Have you tried asking your uncle for a loan?"

"I won't ask Uncle Jake for any more help. I'm almost thirty; it's time for me to stand on my own two feet."

Josh bit his lower lip and looked away from Regan. "Besides ..."

She waited for him to go on. When he spoke again his voice was barely more than a whisper.

"They tell me I found the bodies. I was old enough to understand, but I had no memory of it; I blocked everything out." The color in his face drained. "Only now that I'm living here, I'm starting ... to remember ... things, see things ... my father covered in blood so thick I could barely recognize him."

The hair on the back of Regan's neck stood on end. Josh righted his shoulders and deliberately shivered, as if movement of any kind might break the spell of his memories and chase his visions away. He sat up very straight and continued in a stronger voice. "Uncle Jake is wrong. It's not a good idea for me to live here. I need to sell and get away from this place.

"Okay, Regan, if you want to, you can run out now. You wouldn't be the first," Josh jested lightheartedly, but he remained pale.

"I'll stick around a little longer if you want me to." She wanted to put her arms around him and say, "there, there," but knew if she did it would embarrass him, so she maintained her professional demeanor instead.

"I think there's only one chance to sell your house for what it would be worth if it were any other house. It's counterintuitive and risky, but it just might work."

He put his elbows on the kitchen table and propped up his chin on his hands. "What's your plan?"

"We have to play up your house's past. I'll advertise the house as the scene of a crime and hold a nighttime open house, preferably on a night with a full moon. There's a local group, The Santa Cruz Ghost Hunters, who do readings. I'll ask if they'd be willing to take a look at the house.

"Several of your neighbors have said they've seen something in the woods and at least one neighbor even thinks she's seen a ghost in an upstairs window. I'll use that — maybe even say the house may have a ghost or two — not that I believe in them.

"I know a real estate agent who has a blog about haunted houses who will let me post the listing on it, and I can try to find some paranormal fan sites that will let me advertise the house. The market of potential buyers will be limited, but if I reach the right person or, better yet, people, we may not only find a buyer, but start a bidding war."

He clasped his hands together and rested them on the kitchen table. Regan touched his hands gently, wondering if she had gone too far. "Would you be all right with me doing that, Josh?"

He started to smile again, tentatively at first, but with growing enthusiasm, "I think my research has paid off. You have a reputation, Regan. The story is you're a good realtor who does her job creatively and well. I like your ideas."

Regan returned a small smile, "I do work hard for my clients ..."

"There's more, though," he interrupted. "I know you're the perfect agent to sell this house. I know that because I've also heard you've been involved with murder before."

Regan's direct line rang as she put her purse in her desk drawer and sat down. "Regan McHenry," she answered.

"So, I'm reading the newest post from the International Society for Paranormal Research and I saw your ad on it for a house that has a ghost. I'd like to see it."

The caller was the seventeenth response to her ad. The first sixteen had been looking for adventure, not a house, and Regan was beginning to doubt her marketing strategy. "The ad is for a house for sale, not a haunted house tour."

"Yeah, I understand that. I want to see the house. I'm looking to buy a house. Seeing the ghost would be a definite plus, but not an absolutely necessity. Also, I'm interested in the land. Can I grow crops on the land?"

It was good the caller couldn't see Regan take a deep breath and roll her eyes as she anticipated his answer to her question. This call, she feared, was going to be another strikeout, but for a different reason. "What kind of crops are you interested in growing?" she asked, sure he would say herbs, the standard euphemism for marijuana.

"Grapes. Red wine grapes, although I don't know if I'll go

French and do a Pinot Noir or go with an Italian Sangiovese or a Nebbiolo. In any case, I've got a first draft, well, more of a working doodle of my label: kind of a white swirling apparition holding a big green bottle and spilling red wine from it so it looks like blood flowing. I'm gonna call my brand Ghostly Grapes or Bloody Reds, something like that. The wine will be resolute though: complex and well balanced. Symmetrical. Symmetry is everything."

Regan was relieved his answer wasn't what she expected; still the label he imaged was unsettling. "The zoning allows for growing grapes and there are some open rolling meadows on the property, although much of the land has big redwood stands which wouldn't necessarily …"

He spoke over her, "I could start small with the meadows and take the trees out over time if I need to. I want to see the house. Can you show it to me later today?"

They agreed to meet at the property at three o'clock. Regan offered to drive them from her office, but the caller said he would be coming down the coast from San Francisco and didn't want to come all the way into Santa Cruz. Besides, he said, he wanted to have his off-road vehicle with him so he could drive the land. He had GPS and said he'd find the house. He wasn't daunted when she explained there were no cell towers in Bonny Doon and that he would lose coverage once he left Highway 1 and headed inland from the coast.

Finding the property was a little tricky if you didn't know where you were going. She chastised herself for not insisting she drive as she leaned against her car and fidgeted, waiting as time passed. It was approaching four o'clock before a red Porsche Cayenne pulled up next to her.

"I'm late, I'm sorry. You look seriously ticked," the driver waved a hand apologetically as he slid from the driver's seat and dropped to the ground. "I stopped at the tasting room on Bonny Doon Road. The owner was in — we talked — I had a lot of questions. Then he brought out some private reserve and time got away from me. Will you not be mad at me for being so late when I buy the house?"

"Are you old enough to sign a contract?" Her question was sarcastic enough; she intended to ask it evenly, but her tone matched her words. He was a soft, round boy, no more than five-feet-five-inches tall she ventured as she looked down at him from her five-foot-nine-inches-in-flats vantage point. His hair, such a light blonde that it was almost white, was bowl-cut and he wore enormous black-rimmed glasses perched on pale white cheeks. He reminded her of a baby snowy owl.

This likely game-playing child had kept her waiting for almost an hour. Her question and its delivery reflected just how annoyed she was at him and, more importantly, how annoyed she was at herself for letting him play her.

He didn't seem to notice her ire or her sarcasm. "I get asked stuff like that all the time. I'm twenty-one, actually. I just look like a kid. Can we go see the house now?" he smiled, ready to move on to what mattered to him. "My friends call me Stevie or Bird. You can call me whichever name you like best."

Bird was so tempting. "I'll call you Stevie."

The seller had agreed to leave the front door unlocked and to be gone during the showing. Regan escorted the enthusiastic not-a-kid up the stairs and opened the door. It still creaked forebodingly.

"Nice." Stevie grinned showing tiny teeth which hindered her attempt to see him as a grownup. "Will you point out where the ghost has been seen?"

She decided to go with her customer's frame of mind. "There are two reported ghosts. One is a woman in a red dress that supposedly has been seen upstairs in the master bedroom where the female murder victim was found; the other has reportedly been seen outside, manifesting as a glowing ball of blue light moving through the woods at the side of the house. Some observers say the light turns into a human form ..."

"Oh wow!"

They completed the house tour and were heading outside to look at the land when a car pulled up behind Stevie's Cayenne. The seller and another man got out and began climbing the steps toward them.

Josh acknowledged her with a nod. "Regan, I thought you'd be gone by now. This is my Uncle Jake. We can make ourselves scarce if you like."

Regan shook the older man's proffered hand. "No need, Josh. We're finished with the house. We're going to take a look at the land. This is Stevie Butler. He's looking for a house to buy and likes the idea of it having a ghost or two. Stevie, may I introduce you to the owner ..."

He spoke directly to Josh. "We don't need to look at the

Nancy Lynn Jarvis

land. I already know I want to buy your house. I can already tell the land will work to get me started. I'll just have to have a few trees taken down at the side of the house near the back. You gonna be okay with that?" he asked Josh. "You're not a tree hugger are you? I like the trees, but I'm going to put in vineyards and I want to be able to look out the kitchen windows and see my grapes growing."

"If you buy the house, you can do whatever you want with it; it won't matter to me."

"Cool. What do we do next? Do we sit down and decide everything or what?"

"If you're serious, Stevie, we go back to my office and write a formal offer which I'll present to Josh."

Stevie studied Josh wordlessly. "I'm serious. We'll see more of each other later, I guess." Stevie half bowed toward Josh and his uncle before he started down the stairs to his vehicle.

Josh flashed a silent questioning look at Regan. She raised an eyebrow and shrugged. "We'll see," she said before following Stevie down the steps.

"I'll follow you so I don't get lost," Stevie called out of his car window. He turned on his music; the sounds Regan heard were loud and jarring.

Regan held the office door open for Stevie.

"So are you like the boss of this place?" he asked.

"Kind of."

"Nice."

She walked him down the hall to her office, pointed to a chair opposite her desk, and motioned for him to sit down. She got out a file, took out a stack of papers, and handed them to him. "Read these."

Stevie shuffled through the stack and read quickly.

"You understand that by having me write the offer, I'll be representing both Josh, as the seller, and you, as the buyer. Are you okay with that?"

"Can you do that? I don't mean is it legal, I mean can you?"

"Yes. I just have to remember who I'm representing at any given moment and do the very best I can for each of you. For example, I can't tell you how much less than the asking price Josh might accept for his house, even if I know how much it is. Conversely, I can't tell him what you're willing to pay, even if I know it's more than you're offering."

"I don't want to offer him less than he's asking. And you've told me I can have inspections, but I don't want any. The house is what the house is. If there's something wrong with it, I'll fix it after I own it. Besides, you said he's just redone everything. You've given me copies of the work he did, and the permits for the work he did, and the receipts. I'm good with the house. I don't need any time for inspections."

"You'll need a contingency to secure a loan."

"No, I won't. I have the money."

"You want to make an all-cash offer?"

"Uh-huh."

"Stevie, I'm wearing my buyer hat right now. I'm advising you that you can ask for some concessions from the seller."

"I don't want any concessions. I only want two things. I want to make sure that once he agrees to sell me the house, he has to go through with it, even if he doesn't want to anymore. And I want him to arrange to have the trees I told him about taken down. The trees can be cut after I own the house, but I want to know he doesn't feel bad about me taking them down.

"More important, where I want to take down the trees is kind of where you said one of the ghosts has been seen. I want Josh to be responsible for arranging for their cutting and to pay for their cutting in case the ghost gets mad with the trees being taken out. I don't want the ghost blaming me for anything."

Regan bit her lip to keep from giggling at Stevie's concern. "Don't you want to negotiate anything else?"

"Nope. I want to buy the house. I have plenty of money and I'll make more if I need any. I have lots of ideas."

"Stevie, if you don't mind too much, would you tell me how …"

"I write apps and games. A couple of them are big sellers. I'm kind of rich, I guess, and like I said, I've got more ideas. My parents are having a hard time with me dropping out of high school — I figured having a piece of paper is no big deal if I have money instead, and I was so bored in school. But it really bugs them I left before I graduated. So I got my GED and then enrolled at UC Santa Cruz. I aced my SATs — tests are so easy — so I got in. The school is ranked like number eight in the nation for video game design. I can knock off a degree … even a master's or a Ph.D. if my parents want … while I do what I want to do, which is to be a world-class

18

winemaker.

"Oh, and I'm into ghosts and the paranormal, so I'm gonna combine all my interests." His baby-like teeth filled his smile. "So you just make sure Josh can't not sell once he agrees to, and that if anything happens to him, I can still get his house. That's all I want."

"The contract covers all of that, but to be certain, we can put in additional language that will bind his heirs, survivors, and estate ..."

"Yeah, good. Do that." He looked down and began rubbing the thumb of one hand between the fingers of his other hand. "Don't tell Josh, but when I met him, I got a, well, I got a kind of a bad premonition, which is weird 'cause I've never had one before."

Josh was jubilant. "That's it? All he wants is for me to promise to sell to him regardless of my future and to arrange to take down a few trees? Is he for real?"

"I believe he is. We'll know for sure in a couple of days. He didn't write a deposit check to open escrow, he wrote a check for the entire purchase price. If the check clears, we know he has enough money to buy your house. There will be no inspections, no appraisals. Stevie has already read and signed off on all the disclosures we filled out earlier. All you'll have to do is provide a document stating you have hired a tree removal company and sign your escrow documents. In a week-and-a-half your house will be sold for your asking price."

"Where do I sign? And when can we start looking at beach condos? Wait till Uncle Jake hears; he's going to flip out. When I told him I put the house up for sale, he said I should cancel with you. He still says he wants me to keep the house, but I think he's just saying that because he doesn't think anyone will buy it and he doesn't want me to be disappointed. Wait till he hears. He's going to be amazed!"

"Regan? It's Inez. Tell me about your new Bonny Doon listing. I hear it's the Murder House. Is that true? When are you doing a broker's open house — or are you? Would anyone come?"

Inez was one of those realtors who didn't need to give her last name over the phone. She had been around and had a high profile for so many years that everyone knew her. Almost everyone liked her, too; Regan certainly did.

"Hi, Inez. It is the Murder House. I was planning a broker's open for the first full moon; I planned to do a nighttime event and play up the house's spooky history, but I don't think I'll need to do anything now. The house went into escrow on Saturday."

"For real?"

"Looks like it."

"Who brought the buyer?"

"I'm double ending this one. The buyer called me off an ad."

"Is it a good offer? Close to asking price? How many days till close of escrow? Does the seller have to do a lot of fix-ups?"

"Inez, you know I can't give you any information about the offer."

Inez sighed loudly. She knew Regan wasn't being coy. There were ethics involved and rules to be followed even between friends, but she always tried.

"But, Regan, I've got a new client who wants to write an offer. They're pretty insistent, but I don't want us both wasting time if your offer's going to fly. If you're double ending, I'm sure you'll see that it does. Your offer is probably so good that there's no point in me writing an offer, is there?"

"Nice try, Inez," Regan chuckled. "You know backups are always welcome. That's all I'm going to say. Tell your client to give it his best shot."

"Regan, you are so mean. I'm old and tired and you're making me work hard without even giving me a hint if I'm wasting my time."

Regan laughed out loud. "Indeed. Tell you what, I'll buy you lunch when you bring that offer to kind of mitigate how hard you have to work."

"You've got a deal." Inez sighed again even more loudly and theatrically than she had the first time. "I guess I have to go see the place before I meet my buyer. All the way to Bonny Doon just to do my due diligence for an offer that probably won't work; it hardly seems fair."

"Poor you. I'll see you for lunch when? Today? Or tomorrow?"

"Tomorrow. No, make it the next day. Give me a couple of days to get everything together. It's just a backup offer that probably won't go anywhere and I don't move that quickly anymore."

"I'll be expecting you for lunch on Wednesday, then."

🏠🏠🏠🏠🏠🏠🏠🏠🏠🏠🏠

Inez parked at the foot of the steps leading up to the Murder House. It was a gray day. Rain was expected by nightfall but it was still hours away. She decided against bringing her umbrella with her and started up the steps, muttering softly to herself as she climbed.

"There would be so many steps ... ouch, darned ankle ... it still acts up after that fall when the weather's like this ... probably a touch of arthritis. I should have told that buyer I didn't have time for a new client. All the way to Bonny Doon, and for what? Regan will make sure her buyer gets the house. It's not likely I'll convert this client either ... they only want to buy this house, nothing else. They are willing to go over asking price, though ... I'm sure Regan's buyer isn't near asking ... who would be on this house? Maybe when the seller sees my client's offer, he'll find a way to scare away Regan's buyer ... not likely he'll go, though ... if he's getting a good price."

Inez was slightly out of breath by the time she reached the top level. She felt around in her cavernous purse for her smart phone, retrieved it, and began stroking the phone, performing the steps necessary to gain access to the house, complaining aloud after completing each maneuver.

"It was so much easier when we just had keys to a lockbox ... now it's enter the code, find the box ... get close enough to make it work. All this new technology ... and it changes every time I get used to it.

"Blast it!" she yelled at full voice and then some. "Come on you box. Open!" She tried her phone again with the same result. She continued her tirade, "Cell connections never work properly in Bonny Doon.

"Well, hopefully the seller knows that ... maybe Regan educated him and he left his door unlocked," she muttered to herself as she dropped her phone into her purse again. "I don't even know why I'm still working at my age ... maybe if I close this deal, I'll just call it quits."

As Inez reached for the doorknob, she realized the door was slightly ajar. She called out as she pushed the door open, "I called earlier! Realtor to see the house!"

Her scream began as a moan deep in her throat and rose steadily in volume until it escaped in a shrill outcry. Inez dropped her purse and turned for the steps, screaming in unrelenting waves as she descended, more loudly each time her injured ankle took her full weight.

The killer caught up with her before she was halfway down the steps and pushed her forward just as she was mid-stride to the next step. The push forced her beyond the riser. She landed lower than she expected and off balance. Her ankle twisted sharply as she landed and snapped at the weak point with a sickening sound. She was on her knees and in so much agony she didn't try to defend herself against the rock that smashed her head. Inez probably died under the force of the first blow, but the killer was methodically thorough, hitting her again and again to crush her skull.

Still clutching the bloodied rock, the killer stood upright

over the motionless Inez and looked left and right to see if anyone was coming in response to her cries. No one was in sight. The rock had torn the latex gloves the murderer wore. "Better take you with me," the murderer addressed the rock. "We wouldn't want any of my DNA turning up on you. We'll stop by the beach on our way home, and you can have a nice kerplop in the ocean.

"And as for you," the killer spoke to Inez's corpse, "let's take you inside the house." The killer produced another set of gloves from a back pocket and put them over the torn ones before taking up Inez's ankles. The killer was not large or overly strong; it was a struggle to drag Inez's body up the steps. It took time. The killer had to stop and rest before clearing the top step. "You're heavier than you look."

Inez's body left a bloody trail up the steps as she was dragged and scuffed toward the front door. The killer didn't care. "Let's put you on the foyer floor against the staircase, in the same place where the realtor was found last time, before I take Josh upstairs."

Tom opened Regan's office door and stepped inside. A smile blossomed on her face as she looked up from her computer screen. Even after twelve years of marriage, the sight of her husband, and especially his intense blue eyes, caused her heart to beat a bit faster, and rarely failed to make her happy.

He was normally as pleased to see her as she was to see him, but today he didn't return her smile. He positioned himself in a half-sit on the corner of her desk with his long legs still on the floor.

Dave followed Tom into her office and said nothing as he closed the door behind him. He seemed even more restrained than her husband — unusual for Dave. Still silent and unsmiling, he sat down in one of the chairs opposite her desk.

Dave was her best friend, but observers who didn't know them would never guess that they bickered and teased one another mercilessly, always trying to have the last word. A non-wisecracking Dave was definitely out of the ordinary.

"Don't look so glum, you two. You're friends. I don't mind that you want some private guy-time. I won't be offended that you aren't going to invite me to lunch," Regan teased. "I have plans of my own."

Dave stared at her intently. "Tom and I aren't having lunch together today. I'm here in an official capacity."

"Oh," Regan drawled, "in an official capacity." She raised her eyebrows still expecting Dave to deliver the punch line of a joke made at her expense.

"It's serious, sweetheart." Tom reached for her hand. "There's been another murder — another two murders — at the Murder House."

She glowered at Dave, ready to castigate him for getting her husband to participate in such an abominable joke. Dave's face held no hint of mischief. She looked back at Tom. His eyes were filled with concern.

"Not Josh?" Regan winced as she said his name.

Tom nodded, "And Inez Passaro."

"Inez? No, that's not possible." Regan shook her head. "We're having lunch in about fifteen minutes." She looked toward Dave incredulously; surely he would change his story now that he knew about her plans.

"Their bodies were found early this morning. The coroner says they've been dead since yesterday. Their bodies were arranged to mimic the murders from nineteen years ago."

Regan listened to Dave without truly registering what he was saying, noticing instead that he was still a policeman. Even if he was no longer regularly in the field as such, he still spoke with the detachment cops use for emotional self-preservation.

"Are you sure it's them?" She had just presented him with an opening. Her naïve question should have elicited a snappy quip from Dave.

"There's no question about their identity. He was recognizable. His throat was slit like his mother's was. His uncle's been out of town on business — he just got back into town this morning — and he came straight from the airport to identify the body. Your realtor friend was … well, she's been positively identified. Her purse was there with her ID, and then her boss, her broker, made the call so her daughter wouldn't have to see her. She was pretty damaged."

"What happened to her, Dave?"

Tom tightened his grip on her hand. "Maybe it would be better if I told you later."

"Dave?"

"What we know is preliminary, but it looks like your friend Inez surprised the murderer. Caught him in the act or came in right after he killed the male Vic. It looks like she tried to run down the front steps, tried to get away, but she didn't make it. The murderer likely used a rock from the garden edging. It was an opportunistic kill, not clean like the first murder."

"Dave." Tom frowned his displeasure at Dave's description, trying to silence him, but Dave ignored his warning.

"The blood trail told the story. She was dragged back inside the house and her body was placed in the exact same spot where the realtor was found last time."

Dave was finally quiet. He studied Regan. "You talked to both of them. Maybe they told you something that would give us some insight. The Chief wanted to have you come down to the station for an interview. You know me, I mostly do PR and media stuff now, but I still keep a hand in all sorts of police business, and I'm persuasive. I reminded him how I may have lost my eye in that shootout years ago, but I didn't lose my interrogation skills. I told him that since we're friends, we might accomplish more if you talked to me rather than to an officer you didn't know, and that it would be better if you were in a more familiar setting than the stationhouse.

"So here I am, ready to let you do your part by telling me everything you remember. And Regan, that's all I want you doing; no playing detective this time. Am I making myself clear?"

Regan nodded.

"Good. Let's start with the realtor. Any idea why she was there?"

"Inez said she had a client who wanted to write an offer on the house. She hadn't seen the property yet and, knowing her, she probably felt she had to before she wrote an offer."

"You think she hadn't seen the house? Does that mean she hadn't met the Vic?"

"I guess it does."

"Her client … man or woman?"

Regan thought hard, trying to recall exactly what Inez said to her. "She didn't say. All she said was she had a new client who wanted to write an offer."

Dave produced a pen and a small notebook from the pocket of his trademark Hawaiian shirt, flipped the pad open, and scribbled on it.

"Okay. What can you tell me about your Josh Miller?"

Regan swallowed hard. "He was nice, Dave." She looked up at Tom. "He reminded me of Ben."

29

"We'll ask others, too, but I want to know if you noticed: did he keep his doors locked? I know some of you people who live in the country don't."

"Josh did, I think, at least he did most of the time."

"But not all the time?"

"I put a lockbox on his house. Realtors use smart phones to open the boxes, but cell coverage is problematic in Bonny Doon. I told him that, and he said he would unlock his front door if he knew an agent was going to show the property. He said he'd unlock his front door and then make himself scarce for a while."

Dave added to his notes. "Would he have unlocked his door for your friend Inez?"

"Probably." Regan reconsidered. "Well, maybe not. Inez knew the house was in contract. If she spoke to Josh to make an appointment, I bet she encouraged him to stick around. It would have been like her to try and sound him out about the offer to see if there was anything she could do to upend it. And if she told him she didn't have a client with her, he might have decided he didn't need to leave. Is it important to know if his door was locked?"

"Oh yeah."

"Why?"

"Goes to whether or not the Vic let his killer in. If your Josh guy let his killer in, he probably either knew him or was expecting him."

Regan nodded absentmindedly and Dave noticed.

"Look, I can see you're starting to get that amateur sleuthing itch. Don't scratch it." Dave stared hard at Regan. "Leave the investigation to the police."

He took up his notepad again and positioned his pen, ready for her next answer. "You're always going on about how close you get to your clients. What did Josh Miller tell you that he didn't tell anyone else?"

Regan didn't need any time to think about her response. "He told me he was starting to remember things. He was a child when his mother and Roger Commons, the realtor from before, were killed. Josh said he walked in on the aftermath — saw his father covered with blood — but that he had blocked it out until recently. When he moved into the house, he started remembering things, things that were upsetting.

"I don't think he told that to anyone but me, not even to his uncle, because he said his uncle wanted him to stay in the house. His uncle raised him; they were close. I don't think his uncle would have told Josh to stay if he knew his nephew was troubled.

"Dave, why now?" Regan asked softly.

"What do you mean?"

"Everyone believes Josh's father committed the other murders. Last time he let his son live, even though Josh was a witness to what he had done — the police do think the killer is the same person as last time, don't they? — so why kill him now?"

Dave held up a hand. "I never said anything about our theory of who the murderer is, past or present. Tom, did you hear me say anything about who we think committed these murders?" Dave rushed on before Tom had time to answer. "No, you didn't. Don't go putting words in my mouth, Regan."

"She doesn't have to, Dave. You said Inez's body was in

31

the same place as the realtor's body was last time. Considering she was killed outside and brought back inside the house, her placement had to be deliberate. Who would know where her body should be placed except the original murderer and the police? Isn't thinking the same person committed all four murders just a logical assumption?"

"Like I said, it's too soon to assume anything, logical or not."

Dave had a few more simple questions for Regan and another admonition about not getting involved in the investigation. "I know you liked these people; we'll figure out who killed them," he promised, and then, in an attempt to lighten the mood in the room, he added with a wink, "and you don't need your name in the news again with a connection between you and murder."

"Dave, not now," Tom exhorted.

Regan was pensive after Dave left. "He's right, you know. Josh said as much the first time we met. He said I had a reputation for being in the midst of murder. I'm beginning to feel like a bearer of curses."

"I think you're looking at this in the wrong way. It's not like your presence has invited catastrophe — just the opposite — you've been involved in justice. That's a good thing. Dave's right, though: leave this one to the police."

Regan dreaded the prospect of telling Stevie about the murders, but she picked up the phone as soon as Dave left and Tom finished consoling her about Inez, feeling it was better that Stevie heard about it from her than from some other source. He answered on the first ring.

"Stevie, something dreadful has happened."

"You mean about Josh? Yeah, it sucks. He was cool."

"How did you hear?"

"Some police guy called. I talked to Josh yesterday. My number was on his phone's recent call list. The cops think I may have been the last person to talk to him. How freaky is that? They want to see me. I'm on my way down the coast right now. I'm already almost to Santa Cruz."

"We need to talk, too."

"I can stop by your office after I finish with them if you want me to."

"I think that's a good idea."

"Okay, see you in about an hour, maybe sooner. I didn't talk to Josh for long yesterday so I don't have much to tell the cops. It shouldn't take long."

Nancy Lynn Jarvis

🏠🏠🏠🏠🏠🏠🏠🏠🏠🏠🏠

Stevie didn't arrive until three hours later. He walked into her office, aggravated and sullen, with his hands jammed in his hoody pouch, and slumped into a chair opposite her desk.

"Man, Santa Cruz cops are crazy. For a while they acted like I killed Josh and that woman. They went on and on about how I probably called to set up a meeting to see Josh and then, since he was expecting me, that's how I got into his house. They asked me if Josh was sitting or standing when I snuck up behind him and slit his throat. They showed me pictures of the bodies and asked if that was my handiwork — handiwork: that's the word they used. Gross. Just because I called him — why would I do something like that?"

Regan was taken aback as Stevie spoke, but reached the same conclusion he did: he was an unlikely murder suspect. She was curious about his call to Josh, though. "Why *did* you call Josh?"

"Not you, too!"

"I'm not accusing you of anything; it's just that you were supposed to call me if you had questions, not him. We talked about that."

"You have too many rules. I'll follow rules if they're fair — I like things to be fair — but I won't follow rules just because they're there. I liked talking to Josh, and I wanted to talk to him directly about the trees he's having cut. The guy he hired was supposed to come by today. I wanted to make sure we agreed which trees were coming down. Breaking your no direct contact rule was no big deal.

"I didn't like having to see those pictures, especially not

the ones with the woman realtor all messed up."

"Stevie, I'm sorry for what you've been through. We can get you out of the contract, considering what's happened ..."

"You mean not buy the house?" Stevie's voice shot up an octave. "You said you fixed it so I could buy the house even if something happened to Josh. Didn't you do that?"

"I did put in the language we discussed. I thought after what happened you wouldn't want to continue."

"No — I mean yes — I still want to buy the house. The media hype that's going to come with a second set of murders will be amazing. With publicity like that, I can't wait until my vines start producing. I'll have to buy grapes and settle for bottling on the property so I can get wine with my brand out there if I'm going to take advantage of these murders."

Regan tried not to react as Stevie outlined his plan, but she grimaced nevertheless.

"What?" Stevie shrugged. "Don't go judgmental on me. Being all sad and mopey isn't going to do Josh any good. Besides, you're no different than me. You used the house's history, too, when you advertised the way you did. Carpe diem, right? Or in this case, carpe phasmatis. Seize the ghost. It's my right." He grinned showing an even row of baby-sized teeth.

"I already put my money in and signed the papers the escrow people wanted me to sign. Have you seen the ink they use for your thumbprint? It disappears without staining your finger. How cool is that?"

"Escrow won't close on schedule, Stevie. Nothing is going to proceed on schedule. Josh's death is going to slow things down."

Stevie blinked behind his glasses, his slow owl blink. "For how long?"

"It depends on how his estate is structured. Best case is a couple of weeks, worst case, a few months. Josh's uncle may have some information about Josh's affairs. I'll have to track him down and ask. It may take a while for me to get his phone number."

Stevie produced his phone and stroked it a couple of times. "I have his phone number." He turned his phone so she could read it.

"Why do you have Josh's uncle's number?" Regan asked as she jotted it down.

Stevie returned the phone and his hand to his hoody pouch and shrugged. "I like to keep track of people. I like to see how close we are, you know, it's that six degrees of separation thing. I've got information about you, too." He took his phone out again, stroked the phone screen, and then held the phone out toward her again, inviting her to see her profile.

"I'll talk to Josh's uncle as soon as it's reasonable …"

"Could you call and ask him right now?" Stevie pointed to the phone on her desk.

Regan could feel heat in her cheeks. "Josh's uncle has just lost someone he loved, someone who was like a son to him. Have some compassion. I can't call him today about business, or rather, I won't call him today."

"I told Josh there was no rush about him getting his stuff out of the house. As long as I can move in by the end of the month, that's all I care about. Same deal goes for his uncle. If I buy the house in a couple of weeks, he doesn't have to have

Josh's stuff out right away; he can even leave it for another month if he wants to. That's compassionate of me, isn't it?"

Stevie was on his feet and leaving her office as unceremoniously as he had arrived. He turned back to face her. "I promise I won't call him if you don't want me to. Let me know what he says."

It was almost five o'clock when Amanda, the office receptionist, buzzed her. "Regan, there's a Mr. Miller to see you. Shall I send him back?"

For the briefest moment Regan imagined Josh standing in the front office. Her fleeting sensation ended with the realization that Josh's Uncle Jake must be a paternal uncle who shared the Miller name with his nephew.

"I'll come out, Amanda."

Regan would have known Jake Miller was Josh's uncle even if she hadn't been introduced to him a few days earlier. The family resemblance between them was strong and he was slight like Josh, but his posture was hunched as he stood by the reception desk, something she hadn't noticed about him when they were introduced, and he looked like a senior uncle, an as-yet-unmet older Miller brother, at least a decade older than the last time she saw him.

She took his extended hand in both of hers. "Mr. Miller, I am so sorry. I liked Josh very much; he was a fine young man. You did a wonderful job raising him. After what happened to him, he was fortunate to have you there to love him and care for him."

Regan could feel tears forming in her eyes as she spoke. She blinked to keep them from escaping. Jake Miller was unable to control his. He hastily disengaged her hands and swiped at his cheeks with the backs of both hands. "Thank you."

"Let's go to my office. Would you like Amanda to bring us some tea?"

He shook his head.

"Or some water?"

"No. Nothing, thank you."

Regan took his arm and gently escorted him down the hall, ushered him into her office, and indicated a seat on the sofa rather than the chair opposite her desk. She lowered the blinds on her inside window for privacy before she joined him on the sofa, and then sat silently waiting for him to speak.

He focused on his hands in his lap. "You must think I'm peculiar coming here today ... coming so soon ... I want as much settled as possible ... as quickly as possible. I hope it will help ..." his voice trailed off to a whisper.

"Josh was impressed with your originality, with the way you marketed his house. I know you've spent advertising money and now, with what's happened — I'm certain this, this ... event ... will scare the buyer away — that you won't get paid for your efforts. I want to reimburse you for your expenses. He would have wanted me to do that."

"That's such a kind gesture, and completely unnecessary. It's unwarranted, as well. The buyer has already indicated he wants to continue with the purchase and to do so as quickly as possible."

Jake Miller raised his eyes and stared at her wordlessly. At first he looked uncertain, bewildered, then Regan detected another emotion: Jake Miller was aghast.

"No." He shook his head vigorously. "No, he can't buy the house. The sale has to stop. You have to stop it!"

"It's not up to me." Regan's hands fell open into a pose of helplessness. "The buyer was very specific when we wrote his offer. He wanted language in the contract that made it impossible for the seller to cancel it once it was accepted, language that even obligated Josh's estate to sell in the event something happened to him. I explained all that to your nephew when I presented the offer. Josh agreed to the language as written and approved the contract. At this point, the only one who can stop the sale is the buyer, and he doesn't want to."

"I'm the executor; I'll get an attorney," Josh's uncle sputtered heatedly. "I won't allow him …" His incensed words diminished in force until they became wheezing pants. "You have to stop him … you have to make him understand … it's dangerous to proceed … the house can't be sold. There are ghosts in that house … ghosts of the past."

"Mr. Miller, please calm down. I'll talk to him; I'll try."

Jake's face was ashen; he looked like a ghost himself. "Please," he implored, "the house can't be sold."

Jake Miller sat quietly for a few moments. Though his body was still, Regan could see that his mind wasn't; he searched for understanding.

"These killings … they must mean that my brother has returned. He's killed again in an attempt to stop the sale. You must get the buyer to withdraw; tell him his life may well depend on it. Get him to stop, now."

Regan moved to her desk and dialed Stevie's cell phone number. She was shuttled to call answering. If she knew Stevie, he had stopped by one of the wine tasting rooms near her office before heading back up the coast to his home, and had either turned off the device or, more likely, decided to ignore her call when he saw her name.

"I'll keep trying, but it may be tomorrow before I can reach him."

"Do what you can." A defeated Jake Miller finally seemed drained of all emotion. He wouldn't be walked out; she stood in the hall and watched him go, a man weighed down by dark thoughts and the pain of his losses.

Tom's arm around her waist ended her gloomy observation. "Sandy called. Dave was all business when he interviewed you, but he must have told her about your day. She insisted we come over for dinner and some hand-holding. I told her I should check with you, and then decided that's what friends are for, changed my mind, and said that sounded great. They're expecting us at six." He waited to see if she would protest his decision.

Regan felt as despondent as Jake Miller looked walking down the hall. She had no energy to protest or to turn down an invitation from her best friend and his wife.

"Will there be wine?" She leaned her head against Tom's shoulder.

"It's dinner with Sandy and Dave. Of course there will be wine," he chuckled gently.

"Then we better get going."

"Sandy said she's going to make dinner simple so we can cancel if you don't want to go — she won't mind. You're sure you're up to it? What with Inez and your client, you've had a rough day."

"You don't know the half of it."

He gave her an inquiring look.

"That was Josh Miller's uncle. As executer of Josh's estate, he's my new client by default, so I've had both the buyer and the seller in my office this afternoon.

"Stevie, the buyer, who the police questioned like they think he could be a person of interest in the murders, wants to close escrow ASAP. He's anxious to use the notoriety the murders will cause as publicity for his wine label."

Tom whistled, "Phew."

Regan put her hands on her temples and rubbed. "There's more. Jake Miller, the uncle, is adamant that the sale be stopped. He thinks his bloodthirsty brother — the man everyone agrees killed his wife and a realtor in the house years ago — has returned and is killing again. He believes that Stevie could be his next victim if I don't break the buyer's contract I wrote. Remind me never to double-end a sale again.

"The most interesting part is both of them half-believe the house is haunted because of what's happened there, and I'm almost ready to agree with them."

🏠🏠🏠🏠🏠🏠🏠🏠🏠🏠🏠

Sandy threw her arms around Regan as soon as she opened

the door. "Dave told me what's going on. You must be upset. Come on in — relax."

Dave materialized carrying a full glass of red wine in each hand and gave one to Regan and the other to Tom before they cleared the foyer.

"This should steady your nerves and get you ready for the six o'clock news. Hurry up." He motioned them forward with a wave of his hand and led the way to the family room where the TV was already on and the music introducing the local evening news was playing. "You'll want to see this."

He spoke to both of them but directed his next comment to Regan. "You, or at least your name and the name of your real estate company, made the news again. Your house is the lead story."

"He's right," Sandy nodded regretfully. "We watched the five o'clock feed. Your real estate sign was on screen for several seconds, long enough to be easily read."

The local news opened with a tease for three prominent news reports and then the effusive anchorman announced, "Stay with us for tonight's lead story: The house known to Bonny Doon residents as the Murder House claims two more victims. Stay with us for details when we return."

A Kiley and Associates real estate sign with Regan's name rider affixed to the top filled the screen for several seconds before the program went to commercial. Regan gulped half the contents of her wine glass without tasting it before the screen changed.

Dave let out a whoop. "Your pals in the real estate biz are gonna ask you to give up your license," — the grin on his face grew enormous — "the way you're always lurking around corpses. You don't care if they're fresh or mothballed …" he held up a hand as if to stop the conversation even though he was the only one speaking, "Shhh, they're coming back."

Regan sat tight-lipped as the anchorman related his titillating tale of déjà vu murder, relieved that at least, after the first close-up of their real estate sign, the camera panned back to a shot of the house and her name couldn't be read any longer.

The anchorman, a popular local celebrity, was known for throwing in a bit of humorous commentary with his reporting. As he finished his story, he smiled at his TV audience before he turned to his female co-anchor.

"Here comes the zinger," Dave enthused.

"Erin, is it just my imagination or have we heard real estate agent Regan McHenry's name connected with murder in Santa Cruz before?" the anchorman asked jovially.

Regan drained her glass.

Tom and Sandy did their best to keep the dinner conversation focused on anything except the events of the day; even so, Regan remained silently morose as she ate. By the time they finished dinner, Sandy and Tom had given up their attempt to engage her and had fallen into chatting about the latest in computing and technology, their favorite topics.

"Come on, Regan," Dave cocked his head in the direction of the kitchen. "We'll handle the dishes, won't we? Those two can talk about boring computers all they want."

Once they were in the kitchen, Dave handed Regan a dishtowel. "I'll wash and you dry," he instructed. "I know you're upset about your client and your friend, but you're no fun when you don't take my bait," he grumbled. "I've thrown out some pretty good openers for you tonight. I was ready to let myself take some witty hits from you — and I was so nice to you today, too, not pouncing on some of your dumber comments — but you're not even trying."

Regan responded with a sarcastic, "Your astounding consideration has been duly noted."

"Ah, now that's better," he said cheerily.

"If you're serious about improving my mood, you can do it by answering a couple of questions for me."

Dave squinted his good eye suspiciously. His convincing prosthetic eye, the one that replaced the eye he lost in his traditional-police-career ending gun battle, followed suit. "Okay. Maybe a couple of general questions because I'm such a good friend. What do you want to know?"

"Stevie Butler is my client, too. He came by my office today after meeting with the police. He was shaken up. The police showed him pictures of Inez and Josh and accused him of being their killer. What was that about? They don't really believe Stevie had anything to do with this nightmare, do they?

"My new client by default, Josh Miller's uncle, believes his brother's back and killing again; that's what the police think is happening, isn't it? Why has he come back after almost twenty years? Jake Miller warned me that if Stevie proceeds with trying to buy the Murder House, his life could be in danger, too. What's so remarkable about that house that could elicit murder? Do the police have any ideas about the house?"

"I give you an inch and you push for touchdown yardage.

That's way more than a couple of questions and they're way too specific."

Regan snapped her dishtowel at him.

"We don't think your little pal is going to turn up dead … unless a grape vine strangles him or a ghost gets him."

"The police do think the same person committed all the murders, don't they?"

Dave sucked in his bottom lip and chewed on it. "No comment. I will say our operating theory is whoever did the deed yesterday knew a lot about what happened nineteen years ago … that, and that your Butler kid is one weird guy. He tell you how excited he is about the new murders?"

"Uh-huh," Regan nodded. "But I don't think he's strange so much as completely candid and lacking in social graces. He doesn't filter for how what he says is going to hit a listener's ears the way you and I do."

"No, he's weird. Did he tell you he knew all about the first murders? That's why we liked him for a while."

"He didn't mention that, but he probably researched them. He's one of those kids who spend a lot of time alone with a computer. He's bright, lives in his own world, and delves into all sorts of things on the Internet."

"He's a little ghoul who knows a lot more about the first murders than normal people know, a lot more than normal people would want to know. Looks like he alibied out, though — some friend of his says they were playing video games all day yesterday — so we don't think he killed anyone."

"That leaves Josh's father, doesn't it?" Regan shook her head. "But what kind of man would kill his own son?"

"One who killed his wife and has a big secret to keep."

45

Regan tried to sound upbeat and positive talking to Tom while she stood at the bathroom sink putting on makeup. It was a sham maneuver; she was dreading what she'd be doing for the first half of the day.

"It's an odd place for a memorial service, I agree, but it seems fitting for Inez. There won't be a funeral here — she's being buried near her daughter; her family will be holding one when she's interred — and the Santa Cruz Association of Realtors building has a room big enough to hold everyone expected to pay their respects." She stopped speaking long enough to swipe on lipstick. "Inez was popular and a force of nature when it came to real estate, so she needs a big space."

Tom was at a tricky chin-point in his shaving. "Umm," he grunted his concurrence.

"The title companies all got together and ordered food from Michael's on Main. I've heard the restaurant is donating beverages — Inez used to drop by there for lunch pretty regularly since they're right next door to SCAOR — as their way of honoring her memory."

Regan studied the mascara wand in her hand, reconsidered

her use of it, and put it away unused. "There should be lots of funny stories about her, and some tears, too, I imagine."

"The memorial will do all of you a lot of good — if you get there in one piece, now that you're giving a lift to the dragon lady."

"I can't convince you to come with us?"

"No, you can't. I'll need my car in town later today; besides, she made a big deal out of you driving her. I think she sees the ride to the memorial as an opportunity to get to know you — a become-your-friend kind of excursion. I'd just be in the way."

Regan sighed deeply. "Coward."

"You got that right."

Jackie Donahue — the dragon lady to any real estate agent who knew her before she retired last year unfeted at the age of eighty — had been a truly intimidating figure in her day. She didn't mince words; she minced realtors representing the other side of her transactions. She and Regan had never been close. In fact, their only connection seemed to be that Jackie Donahue lived in Bonny Doon, knew Inez, and wanted a ride to the memorial service. When she called, she didn't ask if Regan would give her a ride, she bestowed the privilege of driving her on Regan. And Regan, because she was polite and not fast enough on her feet to think of a valid reason to turn her down, had agreed to pick her up forty-five minutes before they were due to arrive at Inez's memorial.

"You have one of those cars that looks like every other car you see. I bet the seats are uncomfortable as hell, too," Jackie grumbled as she thrust her cane toward Regan, expecting her to hold it as well as the car door while she maneuvered into shotgun position in Regan's Prius.

Once Jackie Donahue was in, Regan returned her cane, closed the door, walked around to the driver's side, and slid in.

"Not as bad as I imagined," Jackie said as she wiggled in the seat, seeking perfect placement for her boney backside. "But your car still has no style. Give me an '85 Cadillac any day."

Regan cast a sideways glance at her passenger as she maneuvered her car down Jackie's long potholed drive. Jackie appeared in profile, hawkishly staring forward, watching for the potholes Regan couldn't avoid, her beaky nose prominent on her face. To keep from being jostled, she clutched at the car's dashboard with one claw-like hand while bracing her cane against the floor mat with her other hand.

Regan told herself that Jackie wasn't someone intimidating — she was just an old woman, her face grown thin and sharp, her skin fragile and age spotted, and her hands arthritic — but it didn't work. It also didn't help that Jackie, as usual, wore emerald green, Chinese dragon green. Jackie Donahue's innocent infirmities and her choice of favorite color only added to her lore: the dragon lady.

Jackie let go of the dashboard and settled back into the seat once they hit the road. She smiled at Regan, at least that's the way Regan interpreted the look she received; it was that or worry that Jackie was assessing how tasty she might be.

"Are you Irish or is McHenry an acquired name?" Her passenger attacked rather than questioned.

"I'm Irish. I didn't change my name either time I married. My ex was furious about that, but Tom doesn't care."

"I didn't change my name, either. My late husband was a Schwartz." Jackie's smile flirted with exuding pleasure, although it still looked more like a snarl than anything friendly. "And I always sport some emerald green in keeping with my heritage. You should, too."

Regan's favorite color was red. She smiled weakly and without comment.

"You know," Jackie resumed in a chatty manner, "nineteen years ago, I almost listed that house where the murders happened. I knew the owners, the Millers. He had me do a listing presentation, but then he felt I was getting on in years and he needed more 'vigorous representation'. Fool John Miller gave the listing to that philanderer, Roger Commons." Jackie pulled her thin lips back into a derisive sneer. "If he'd given it to me, none of this would have happened."

"Or you could have wound up dead like Roger Commons did," Regan offered.

Jackie glared at her like she was the dumbest woman who had ever walked the earth. "How do you figure that? John Miller could never have caught *me* in flagrante delicto with his wife, now could he?"

"Is that what happened?" Regan probed. "I heard that Roger came in and caught the Miller man either killing his wife or disposing of her body."

"Of course that's what happened," she snapped. "Roger Commons tried to bag almost every woman he met — and when he decided to, he was successful most of the time — I thought you knew that little womanizer. You called him Roger and you've been in the business long enough to have met him, haven't you?"

"I have. I got my license when I was barely twenty-two, and I did run into him once or twice, but I didn't know him, not more than in a passing 'Hello' way."

"Lucky you. I don't know how his wife put up with him; I'd have killed him if I were her. She was probably relieved when he was murdered. If you had been around him more, he probably would have tried to get to know you in the biblical sense … or maybe not … he was a short man so he liked his women petite, and you're a tall drink of water. Why, he once told me, if he'd been twenty years older, he'd have been after me.

"No, John Miller caught his wife and Roger Commons in the act, or at least in such a compromising position there was no doubt what they were up to." Her statement concluded with finality and Jackie leaned back until her head was against the headrest.

She swiveled her head in Regan's direction. "I told you I knew the Millers, didn't I?"

"Yes, you did."

"June Miller worked for one of the title companies for a while, so I'd met her. Not the brightest bulb, not unpleasant, though, and rather pretty; and I knew John from church — we both attended Bonny Doon Presbyterian — me, some for my beliefs, some for the connections it provided, and him —

well, he relished having the reputation of being a good Christian man.

"I knew him well enough that he told me about his bastard son and about why he needed to sell the house. I figure you ought to know all the details since the second murders happened on your watch. That's why I asked you to give me a lift today."

Regan spun her head toward her passenger. Jackie Donahue seemed poised to give her a gossipy history lesson. She hadn't expected *that* when she agreed to chauffeur the dragon lady.

"The first part, the part about old John being cuckolded, he told to me many years ago under the influence of alcohol. My late husband and I were invited to the Gilbert's house for dinner. Did you know them? They moved away … must have been twenty-five years ago; I sold their house. The Millers were invited, too. I remember thinking how stiff John and his wife were with one another; I think she had just told him she had had an affair. He got blootered, cornered me on the back deck, and unloaded."

Jackie let out a cruel chuckle. "I think he regretted telling me the minute he sobered up, but I heard about it again from someone else, I can't remember who right now, though, so it's not like I was the only one he told.

"John Miller fancied himself a saint. According to him, when his wife discovered she was pregnant, she confessed to him that she couldn't be sure the child in her womb was his because she'd been carrying on behind his back. She told him the affair was over and that she would end her pregnancy if he wanted her to and make a fresh start with him.

"He wouldn't hear of it. Oh no. He said he told his wife that, since there was a possibility the baby was his, they'd keep the child and he'd raise it as his own. Smug pain-in-the-ass must have felt so righteous and upstanding." Jackie's beady eyes glistened with the delight of telling her tale.

"The child came out a boy who had John's coloring and slight build and his mother's eyes and mouth, and John did what he said he'd do.

"You know people tell their realtors things they don't share with others; you've had that happen to you, I'm sure."

Regan agreed with a nod.

"Well that could have been why — or maybe it was our church connection — anyway, when he had me by for the listing presentation, he told me his private business, and this time stone sober.

"John said that until a couple of months before, he had believed his wife, believed that she was being faithful. He didn't say so, but I think he even settled into believing the boy was his for sure; but then he started noticing little things his wife was doing that made him think she was up to her old ways.

"He told me that's why he was going to sell the house. He wanted to move her away from Santa Cruz, all the way to the east coast, and get her away from temptation. I bet he told that philanderer all about his heartbreak, too, when he talked to him about listing the house. Imagine what that must have been like for Roger Commons, him being the guilty party in June Miller's past and having to keep a straight face … or maybe John didn't say anything … maybe men don't admit that sort of thing to other men. Who knows?

"The irony was John Miller never knew who his wife's lover was until after he hired that adulterous Roger Commons. What a shock it must have been when he realized he was being deceived by the man he hired for more 'vigorous representation.' Serves him right for not hiring me. He got a broker with real vigor, all right," she snickered in more of a cackle than a laugh, but her voice was filled with genuine amusement, "vigorously in pursuit of his wife."

"Jackie, what you say may explain the first murders, but why would John Miller come back now and kill his son and Inez?"

"Inez, poor thing, was in the wrong place at the wrong time."

"And Josh?"

"Maybe John took a look at his suspect son all grown up now and realized he looked more like a Commons than a Miller. In my opinion, John Miller is finishing up his business. That's why I'm warning you that John is back. If you talk to old timers, they'll tell you they still have a hard time believing he did what he did, but I don't. I saw him drunk. I heard the rage in his voice when he told me about his cheating wife. And now these new murders. Any man who could do what he did is full of rage and passion. He killed once, he could do it again.

"I don't know what he has in mind for his house. Maybe he wants to burn it to the ground with hell's fire, or maybe he wants it to stand empty and be whispered about as a warning to adulterers. Whatever he has planned, make sure you stay out of his way or you could end up like Inez."

Jackie closed one eye in a wink, looking more like a

dragon than ever. "We Irish realtors stick together, that's why I'm warning you about John Miller."

"Not that I don't welcome having my wife grace my office," Tom grinned, "but I thought you were going to work from home the rest of the day after you finished your memorial service and taxi run."

"That was my plan." Regan assumed the stereotypical position of a patient at her psychiatrist's office as she reclined on Tom's sofa.

"But?"

"But the dragon lady … I've got to stop calling her that. Yes, she's bitter and more than a little self-centered, but she's not scary once you get past how she looks and how she bosses people around, and she's a wealth of gossip about the Murder House. I couldn't wait to tell you."

"Tom," Amanda's voice came over the speaker on his phone, "is Regan in there with you?"

"Yes, Amanda, I'm here," Regan called out loudly enough to be heard on the speaker-phone.

"There's an attorney representing Jake Miller here to see you."

They could hear a crisp voice commanding Amanda, "Tell her I will be seen now, please. My business with her is time sensitive."

Tom responded, "In that case, please show him to my office."

Regan sat up and moved to one of the client chairs near Tom's desk. "My tale will have to wait."

Amanda appeared within moments followed by a silver haired man in a three-piece suit. His shirt cuffs hit at precisely the correct point where his wrist met his hand. He wore a clubby silk tie of the most current fashionable width. His shoes were slip-on and, Regan guessed, Italian. Their visitor was overdressed for Santa Cruz: his outfit screamed San Francisco law firm.

"Mrs. McHenry." He held out a manicured hand to Regan, shook her hand, and then offered his hand to Tom. "Mr. Kiley? You are Tom Kiley, the owner of this company and Mrs. McHenry's broker, aren't you?"

"Co-owner. Mrs. McHenry is my partner."

"Jackson Pedrone with the San Francisco office of Lathman and Watson. Very great pleasure to meet you."

Tom hadn't mentioned they were married. She could tell her husband was in guarded mode, giving out as little information as possible and she knew why. Sometimes the presence of an attorney in his office caused him to behave like that. An attorney they both disliked before he even opened his mouth prompted Tom to immediate mistrust and circumspection. Regan wrinkled her nose at Tom behind the attorney's back.

"How can we help you, Mr. Pedrone?"

The attorney turned to face Regan and answered Tom's question as if she had asked it. "It's I who can help you, Mrs. McHenry. Real estate law is my sub-specialty and my first love. I've reviewed the contract you wrote — nicely done. It seems you did an excellent job representing Mr. Butler. I do wonder, however, how well you represented your other client, Mr. Joshua Miller.

"Did you fully explain the implications of the contract he signed, especially how his estate might be affected in the event of his demise? Did he understand those implications? It seems logical that he may not have. Considering that his uncle and he were close, might it not be assumed young Mr. Miller would have wanted to give his uncle discretion and flexibility should he inherit the property? Do you have any witnesses who heard your explanation of the contract to him?

"I'm sure your representation of the seller was exemplary. It's just that sometimes details get confused under scrutiny in a courtroom. Damages can be awarded out of all proportion if it seems an error was committed ... not that I'm saying that's what would happen in this case.

"Fortunately, because of Jake Miller's generosity, there's no need to be concerned about any sort of litigation. As he has told you, Mr. Miller is concerned about the safety of Mr. Butler, should he attempt to move this transaction forward. Mr. Miller understands you have done your utmost to convince Mr. Butler to cancel the contract, but to no avail. Mr. Miller still worries, which is why he consulted me about his options.

"I'm fond of win-win outcomes and so is Mr. Miller. He has authorized me to have you contact Mr. Butler and offer him twenty-five thousand dollars if he agrees to terminate the purchase contract. I understand Mr. Butler is young, just starting out in life, and a windfall like that could prove helpful to him."

"Let me make certain we are all on the same page, Mr.

Pedrone," Tom interrupted. "You are threatening Mrs. McHenry, and by extension our company, with nuisance litigation unless she convinces her client to withdraw, something he has made quite clear he does not want or intend to do? Is that the gist of what you just said?"

Mr. Pedrone smiled and arranged his face in a well-practiced expression of affability. "More or less."

Regan was aware of pain in her hands. As Mr. Pedrone spoke, she had balled her hands into such tight fists, her fingernails threatened to cut into her palms. "Of course, I'll relay your offer to Mr. Butler — I assume you have a written offer because you know the value of a verbal agreement isn't worth the paper it's written on — but I wouldn't be too optimistic if I were you or Mr. Miller. You haven't done your homework on Mr. Butler, have you? He likely won't be tempted by twenty-five thousand dollars."

Mr. Pedrone took a document from his breast pocket and produced a pen. He made a show of crossing out a line on the paper and writing in above it and then handed the document to Regan.

"Ahh. Very good job again, Mrs. McHenry. I see you are quite the negotiator. I'm authorized," he nodded toward her, "in writing, to raise Mr. Miller's offer to fifty thousand dollars. And do bear in mind that I'm not construing your lack of enthusiastic commitment to the original offer as you once again favoring Mr. Butler over Mr. Miller."

Although his voice remained even and calm, Tom's blue eyes had taken on the darker than normal hue that Regan knew meant he was extremely angry. He rose from his desk, went to his office door, and held it open. "I believe our

57

business is concluded. And please don't misconstrue my holding the door for you, Mr. Pedrone, as in any way a friendly act."

The attorney feigned shock at Tom's words but moved toward the open door. "I'm disappointed in you, Mr. Kiley. You seem to be taking our discussion personally, when it is, of course, only intended to be about business."

He hesitated at the door and turned toward Regan. "Oh, and if Mr. Butler refuses this final offer, please advise him that Mr. Miller will be availing himself of all the legal estate settlement channels our firm will devise. Don't you wonder, like I do, Mrs. McHenry, if Mr. Butler will prove to be a patient young man or if he'll get bored during months of waiting for title to clear, and if you could best serve his interests by finding him another suitable property to purchase?"

🏠🏠🏠🏠🏠🏠🏠🏠🏠🏠🏠

Regan did her due diligence for both of her clients by immediately phoning Stevie about Jake Miller's offer. She relayed the threat Mr. Pedrone had delivered, as well.

"This is kind of fun; it's kind of like we're playing a bluffing game. Patience has nothing to do with anything. I want my house. Besides, I like playing games and I like winning them."

"Stevie, you don't have to ..."

"You can tell Josh's uncle that my plan is to buy the house and the ghosts in it. You can tell him, too, I'll up the price by fifty thousand dollars if he lets me move in and start producing wine within the next month, okay? Tell him it's his move."

She could hear Stevie's gurgly little laugh and imagined him flashing his baby-toothed smile. She might have underestimated him. He was much like his owlish looks: wide-eyed and round, but under his soft exterior, he was a determined hunter and tougher than he looked.

When she relayed Stevie's offer to Jake Miller, his reaction to Stevie's gambit was unexpected as well. Rather than issuing not-so-veiled threats like his attorney had done, and like Regan expected him to do, he once again became the distraught man she had seen in her office a few days earlier.

"This is my fault. I shouldn't have gone to Lathman and Watson. It's just that they are one of the most highly rated legal firms in the Bay Area. I thought if I got the best ... I'm not assertive enough ... I thought if a dynamic, experienced attorney represented me ... that he might come up with a persuasive way of easing the Butler boy out of the picture.

"Now everything has gone wrong. I could tell when I talked to Pedrone that he might push too hard ... I should have cut him loose — I do apologize for how he spoke to you and your husband — but I was intimidated by him.

"Mrs. McHenry, please help me. This isn't a game, even though the boy seems to think it is. My brother is capable of ... such cruelty ..." He sighed as his voice trailed off in an unfinished admonition.

"Maybe we can convince John that he's won; I believe he's watching. I will quietly stall the sale. Please take down your real estate signs and stop any advertising of the property.

Make everything look like the house is no longer for sale and is abandoned again like it was before I gave it to Josh … if only I hadn't encouraged him to live there. And tell that fool boy to stay away!" His final words were barely louder than a whisper. "Tell everyone to stay away."

🏠🏠🏠🏠🏠🏠🏠🏠🏠🏠🏠

Regan couldn't remember seeing a traffic backup on Highway 1 near Bonny Doon Road since before the southbound turn lane had been added. When fog blanketed the road, drivers had been known to overshoot the abrupt turn and run off the road, or miss seeing a car coming in the other direction as they negotiated the turn too quickly. There had been crashes, even some fatalities, but not since the turn lane had been built. The day was fog-free and sunny and visibility was good even as daylight slowly faded to dusk, so Regan wondered what had caused the slowdown.

She debated turning around, postponing the removal of her lockbox until another day — Jake Miller asked her to clear out her real estate paraphernalia; he never said she had to do it immediately — but she had already traveled more than ten of the eleven miles from her office to the road leading to the Murder House. She was so close; she kept going even though her speed was so slow it didn't register on her speedometer.

Just as she reached her turn at Bonny Doon Road, an ambulance rolled past with lights flashing and sirens blaring, heading toward Santa Cruz and Dominican Hospital. That explained it: someone must have been hurt farther up the highway.

The stall had cost her more than half an hour and the daylight. It was dark by the time she reached the Murder House, inky dark because the night was moonless; but she had a tool kit in the back of her car with a decent flashlight that would give her enough light to find her lockbox and remove it.

She had retrieved the flashlight and closed her hatchback when she noticed a light moving through the woods. It traveled from the back corner of the house, going left through the sentinel trees, moving at a slow steady speed, flickering in intensity as it passed behind individual trees.

The glow appeared to be floating like the ball of ethereal radiance the neighbors had described seeing at the Murder House — the ghost in the woods, as they called it.

Regan didn't believe in ghosts and she was a curious woman. She flicked on her flashlight and aimed it in the direction of the light, determined to see what the real cause of the ghost light was.

Disappointment hit her at once. While the light from her flashlight brightened the area directly in front of her, it didn't penetrate deeply enough into the woods to reach her quarry, the mysterious light.

Regan needed to move closer if she was going to see anything, but she was hardly dressed for an after-dark woodland trek. She had worn pants to Inez's memorial service earlier in the day — dressy pants, though, worn over stiletto-heeled pumps that were hardly suited for anything but indoors, smooth sidewalks, or possibly the bricked patio landings that ascended from where she was parked to the lockbox on the front door of the Murder House.

The heels of her shoes gave her trouble as soon as she started across the lawn. They became impossible hindrances once she hit the forest floor detritus of fallen redwood fronds and twigs. Regan raised and lowered her flashlight in sweeps, aiming down to see what hazards her next step might bring and then up toward the ball of light, alternating between watching her step and watching the woodland light.

She hadn't gone more than ten feet into the woods when she noticed the light had stopped moving. A moment later it abruptly disappeared. She was undaunted. She had a good sense of direction and was confident that, even in the dark woods, she could find the spot where she had last seen the light.

Her inquisitiveness drove her forward; her spirit was willing, her shoes were not. With her next step, her right heel became mired in an especially soft and deep mound of fallen debris. She clenched her shoe with her toes and attempted to pull it free. Her foot came out of the shoe, but her pump remained where it was.

"Damn!" she swore.

The shoe trap had stopped her forward movement. Except for her solitary expletive, the woods at night should have been quiet and still, but they weren't. Regan could hear crunching and the rustle of tree branches which were being made, not by some apparition, but by a solid entity. Her woodland companion was still a ways off, but coming in her direction rapidly.

She flicked off her flashlight in the hope of hiding her location as her heart began to race. Her curiosity and benign explanation of the causes for the light in the woods vanished in a flash, replaced by sinister images of John Miller.

She had no idea what he might be doing outside the Murder House at night and no idea what he looked like, but filled with sudden apprehension as she was, she placed him in the woods not more than thirty feet from her. Her imagination gave him a face, filled him with murderous rage, and set him rushing at her. She abandoned her other shoe, and though every step hurt her shoeless feet, she ran through the woods toward her car.

She dove inside and locked all the doors with a left-handed press of a button. Her keys remained on the passenger seat where she had left them; she was still clutching the flashlight in her right hand. She turned it off and dropped it on the passenger seat, ready to exchange it for her keys, but the exchange didn't go smoothly: the flashlight knocked the keys to the floor.

In her haste to grab the keys and start the car, she wound up slowing her progress and costing herself time. She forgot all about the flashlight as she bent to retrieve the keys, feeling around in the dark for the illusive objects … until she began to laugh at herself.

She had lived in Bonny Doon for more than a decade; she knew how squirrels leaping through trees could sound like giant birds of prey. She remembered how she screamed when Harry, their adopted cat, rubbed against her legs as she and Tom walked garbage cans up their long driveway the night they had seen Jurassic Park in 3D, convinced in that instant that they were about to be attacked by a pack of velociraptors. And she was certainly familiar with what innocent deer sounded like as they moved through the woods at night.

She had heard too many stories of the menacing John Miller recently. He had insinuated himself in her mind and taken over her thoughts; she hoped her favorite dressy pumps hadn't paid the price for her silliness.

Regan found her keys and inserted the car key into the ignition — retrieving her shoes and removing the lockbox was definitely going to wait for daylight — and reflexively turned to check for traffic as she turned the key. She saw a dark figure, very much human, out of the corner of her eye.

Regan floored the gas pedal; her car leapt forward an instant before something smashed into it. The support structure between the driver's window and the back window took most of the blow's force; even so, the safety glass in both windows exploded into hundreds of pebbly pieces.

Her attacker's second swing shattered her hatchback window. She cringed, but kept her foot firmly on the gas pedal, gaining speed as she descended the Murder House driveway.

Her Prius bottomed out where the driveway angled up onto the road. Her tires squealed and her car wobbled from side to side. She crossed the central yellow line and swerved dangerously close to a tree on the opposite side of the road before regaining control of her car.

Regan hadn't screamed during the attack. The blows had come with such violence and speed she hadn't had time for any reaction except flight. But as she sped for home, the realization of what had just happened caught up with her. She screamed into the night, panting, and gulping the cold air blowing through her shattered windows.

She gradually grew calmer as she put distance between herself and the dark figure at the Murder House, but she was still shaking when she reached home. Regan abandoned her car in front of her house, leaving the damaged driver-side door ajar, and ran for the safety of home, not stopping until she was inside.

"Tom!" she cried out, "Tom, I've got to call Dave. I've got to call the police. John Miller just tried to kill me!"

"You go for walks in these things?" Dave asked as he slid open the door from their courtyard and let himself into their house. "They don't look like good hiking shoes to me."

"I wasn't hiking." Regan cradled the pumps Dave held toward her, inspecting the stiletto heels closely. Except for a little loose dirt, they appeared none the worse for their adventure in the woods.

"Oh, that's right. You weren't hiking, you were doing a little ghost chasing, weren't you?"

"How did you find them in the forest at night?"

"I didn't. A deputy sheriff found them. Can we sit in the kitchen so I can take notes?" As he followed Regan into the kitchen, Dave began whistling the theme from *Ghost Busters* just loudly enough to be sure she could hear him.

"Funny," Regan said acerbically, "I was attacked, Dave."

"Yeah, that was pretty obvious. She okay, Tom?"

"She seems to be. I am pouring a glass of brandy to steady Regan's nerves, though, and because she shouldn't be drinking alone, I was pouring one for me, too. How are your nerves tonight; are you in need of a glass of medicinal brandy?"

"I think so — tense drive all the way up here in the dark." Dave held out a hand and feigned shaking.

Dave took the offered glass and swirled its contents. "Tell me what you were doing in the middle of the night at the place where a couple of murders took place by person or persons unknown just a few days ago? And you better not say you were playing detective after I told you not to."

Dave scolded, but he was teasing her, a sure sign he was relieved to see that she, like her shoes, was unscathed.

"It wasn't the middle of the night, and I wasn't playing detective. I was being a conscientious realtor, collecting my lockbox as instructed by one of my clients."

"You hang your lockboxes in the woods, do you?"

"Don't be sarcastic."

"It's a fair question, Regan," Dave said.

"I saw a light in the woods. I was trying to see what it was."

Dave knotted his face into a look of disgust. "I took a look at your car on the way in; if that guy's reach had been a few inches longer, it would have been your head that took the force of that blow. You had no business at that house tonight."

"I looked at Regan's car, too. It wasn't hit with a branch or anything the attacker picked up in the woods, was it?" Tom asked.

"Not likely. We think the weapon of choice was something metal — best guess, a crowbar or a shovel. We'll know more in the morning after one of our crime scene guys takes a look at Regan's car."

"Which means Regan's attacker had a crowbar or a shovel with him when he went into the woods, right? So the question becomes what would someone be doing in the woods at night that required the use of one of those implements that was so secret they'd try to kill Regan to conceal it?"

Dave shrugged, "Good question. No answer. Now Regan, can you give me a description of the guy who bashed your car? What did your attacker look like?"

"I can't tell you how tall he was, or the color of his hair, or if he was young or old. In all fairness, I can't even say for sure if he was a man or a woman or a ghost; he was just a dark figure that I glimpsed for a second on a dark night. I can't describe him, but I can tell you who he was."

"Oh yeah? Don't keep me in suspense — who was it?"

"John Miller. I'm sure it was John Miller."

7

The younger man let his chain saw dangle from his hand; both he and the tool looked tentative. The older man held his chin in his hand and squinted at the trees while he rocked from side to side, pondering. "We're getting a late start but I figure we can still knock this job out before it gets dark."

"You think we should, boss?"

"I expected that tape to be down by now. It's been up for days; it's gotta be for the house, though, not the woods. Eee-yeah, I think it's okay if we take down the trees."

"If you say so." Except for tugging at his ear, a movement he made without thought when he was nervous, the younger man didn't move.

"Josh sprayed an orange X on the trees he wanted out before he got killed. I took a count. We need to drop seven big guys and a dozen thirty-footers or less. Let's cut 'em as close to ground level as we can. I got the stump grinder and the chipper parked out in the meadow beyond where we'll be workin'. We fell, buck the limbs, and roll the trees along the sides where we cleared — kinda make a nice edgin' trim — and then I'll bring in the grinder and then the chipper to clean up. We should make quick work on the cleanup, be finished before dark, easy."

"You sure it's okay?"

"I just said so, didn't I? The law eatin' at you?"

"Not the law, boss."

"What then?"

The younger man jerked his shoulders up sharply. "I dun know. The ghost maybe."

The older man snorted. "You believe that stuff?"

"I dun know. Maybe. A lot of people think there's a ghost livin' in these woods."

"Well, I don't. Let's get to work; I'm gonna feel a lot better after we finish this job."

"Why's that?"

"Josh paid me cash for the work before he died. I don't feel right about takin' his money and then not doin the job the day I said we would; 'course we didn't because of the murders and the tape, not for lack of bein' willin'. Still, it feels like stealin' from the dead, letting the job go this long."

"Like grave robbin'?"

"No — we're not robbin' a grave; we're not messin' with a body — but it feels like it's not honest to take a man's money and then let a little thing like yellow tape keep us from doin what I said we'd do.

"Come on. Let's start with that big tree near the house." The older man motioned toward a tall tree with a bright orange X on it. "We can go fast — won't need to use any ropes to aim, just some wedges — if one of the big trees knocks a small one down, it won't matter."

The younger man flipped his ear guards into place against

the chainsaw noise and pulled the saw's starter cord. He took a deep breath and let it out slowly, looking left and right before he let his saw bite into the tree.

The loggers felled, bucked, and rolled more than half the trees before they took a lunch break. The sun had moved from directly overhead to slightly west, beginning its slow descent to the horizon, although there were a good six hours of daylight left before nightfall. The men sat on one of the logs they'd rolled into place for edging, with the sun at their backs, wolfing sandwiches and downing sodas so as not to take too long before returning to work.

The older man announced he had finished eating and drinking with a loud belch. "I gotta take a leak and then I'm ready to get back to work." He poked his assistant with an elbow. "We want to finish up before dark so the ghost doesn't come out and get us," he teased. He flipped his legs over the log and ambled into the woods a few steps for privacy.

The younger man finished his apple, stood up, wound up like the pitcher he'd been in high school, and flung the apple in an attempt to set a new personal best for core tossing distance. He watched closely to see where the fruit landed. When the core touched down, it broke into two pieces; one part stopped and the other bounced and rolled until it came up against a tree root that had popped above ground when one of the taller trees had dislodged a smaller tree as it fell.

If he marked the core where the first half landed, his pitch wasn't a good one. If, however, he measured from where the second part landed — he smiled to himself — it could be a new personal best. He strode in large even steps in the direction where he last saw the core, counting each step. *It's gotta be around here somewhere …*

"Boss," the younger worker said softly. Then he raised his voice to a shout, "Boss!" His breathing grew rapid and he screamed, "Boss!"

"What 'cha yellin' about?" the older man's irritation was apparent as he jogged to his helper's side.

The young logger pointed to the ground a few feet in front of where he stood. His voice was high pitched with nerves when he answered. "Boss, I think maybe we are grave robbers."

When the small tree was pushed over, its shallow roots broke the surface of the forest floor in several places, bringing everything that was above the roots to the surface as well. The top portion of a rounded skull down to below an eye socket was visible. More disturbing was the skeletal hand near it. Its fingers curved against the dirt like it was trying to use the land as a purchase to help pull itself from its dank resting place.

"Oh, hell, that's not good," the older man grimaced. "Maybe I was wrong about that tape and the sheriff's gonna take my head off. In any case, looks like we're not gonna finish up today after all."

Regan was stirring risotto, an unending and uninteresting chore, with her back to a small TV in the kitchen. She had the local news on for distraction as she performed her mundane task. She had switched to the competing station after her favorite anchorman poked fun at her a few days before about being involved in so many local murders, but she missed him. When they weren't at her expense, his comments usually were witty, so she had switched back for the night's broadcast.

"Well folks, looks like Bonny Doon's Murder House has coughed up another victim. Our Kelly O'Brien is with Officer Dave Everett, who is filling in tonight for the Sheriff's Department spokeswoman. Kelly."

Regan spun to face the TV.

"Thanks Pete. Officer Everett, could you tell us what happened today?"

"Sure, Kelly, be glad to. Two workmen were taking out trees at a property in Bonny Doon …"

"The notorious Murder House?"

Dave smiled at the reporter. Regan thought he looked rather patronizing. "If that's what you want to call it, Kelly. In the course of their work, they unearthed a human skeleton. The County Coroner has taken possession of the remains. Tests will be conducted to determine the sex of the deceased and, if possible, the cause of death and identity of …"

Kelly thrust her microphone even closer to Dave and fairly quivered with enthusiasm as she interrupted his comment. "Does the Sheriff suspect foul play?"

Dave swiftly leaned his head back a few degrees as if he suspected Kelly might attack him with the mic if she didn't like his answer. "I wouldn't want to speculate on that, Kelly. We'll have a lot more information after the Coroner completes his investigation. I'll get back to you, or my Sheriff's Office counterpart will, when she gets back from vacation."

"Officer Everett, is it true the Sheriff was called to the Murder House last night because of an attack on a real estate agent?"

"You'll have to ask the Sheriff about that. I don't follow day-to-day activities at the Sheriff's Department." Dave let a benign smile tip up the corners of his mouth. "That's all for today. Thanks, Kelly."

Regan counted four Kellys in the short interview, a sure sign that Dave was trying to sound relaxed and friendly in spite of his irritation.

Regan traded her stirring spoon for a handset and pressed Dave's home number as soon as his interview ended. His phone only rang twice before he greeted her with, "Ahh, Regan, I was expecting to hear from you. My interview's been over for at least a minute; you're dialing finger doesn't move as fast as it used to, now that you're past forty. So, you calling to thank me for not mentioning your name in reference to what happened last night?"

"Umm, okay."

"Don't overdo expressing your gratitude."

"If I don't seem as grateful as you think I should be, it's because I didn't get a heads-up call. If my clients saw the news and I didn't, I'd seem pretty inept when they called me, which," Regan sighed loudly, "I'm sure they'll be doing any minute now."

"Hey, I've got more to do with my time than to be your personal updater."

"Being the police ombudsman and media interface doesn't seem like a demanding way to earn a living, but I guess doing double spokesperson duty — you poor overworked man — has taken its toll on you because normally you wouldn't be able to resist calling me and rubbing in another calamity near me. So tell me what really happened today?"

"What happened is what I said to the delightful Kelly. Skeleton found. Identity and cause of death unknown."

"Who do you think the body is?"

"How would I know? Remember I just stand in front of the cameras in my colorful Hawaiian shirt and make nice."

"Come on, Dave, what's the theory at the Sheriff's Department?" Regan pursed her lips and gasped as a thought occurred to her: "Do they think I interrupted a burial last night? Is that what the figure in the woods was up to?"

"Not likely. Looks like the guy was in the ground for a while."

"See, you do know what the thinking is. Spill."

Dave made a grumbling noise before he spoke, but he did as Regan asked. "Seems your Josh guy paid these workers to take out some trees before he got killed. They're honest men; rather than just pocketing the money and slacking off, they were determined to do the job they were paid for. The problem was, every time they came by to cut trees, there was crime scene tape up. They got tired of waiting and ignored it today. They brought up the remains with a downed tree. The Sheriff says definitely murder. No idea who the Vic was, but probably a man.

"You remember that drug deal that went bad a few years ago? We know there was a killing, but no corpse was ever found. Remember? Sheriff invested a lot of his deputies' time lookin all over Bonny Doon for a body on a tip. They'll be checking dental records; could be that guy just turned up."

"Why would he be at the Murder House?"

"Well, think about it. If you wanted to get rid of a body, what better place to plant it than in the woods by an abandoned house, especially a house with a reputation and some ghost sightings. It's not like locals would go poking around in those woods, is it?"

"You don't think the body that was found is connected to the other murders?"

"How could it be?"

The odor of singed rice suddenly filled Regan's nostrils. "Oh no!" She grabbed the measuring cup filled with broth and unceremoniously dumped some of it into the risotto. "I think I just ruined dinner."

"I'll let you go see if you can salvage it then, and because I'm such a great guy, I'll probably give you a heads-up on who was in your forest when we identify the remains."

"Is that a promise?"

"It's a promise," he said, pretending to be reluctant. "That'll make two you owe me just this month."

Regan hung up and stirred frantically. Her mind turned over what Dave said almost as quickly as her wooden spoon whirled. He seemed sure the remains weren't related to the other murders. What he said made sense. So why couldn't she shake the feeling that they were, that all the murders were somehow connected?

She put the delicate scallops intended for the risotto back in the refrigerator and took out a few links of highly spiced Andouille sausage and red and green bell peppers. Perhaps if the risotto became Cajun-inspired, Cajun hot with slightly smoky undertones …

Regan's improvisation and pondering was interrupted by the ring of her office phone. It was likely to be Stevie or Jake Miller calling. She didn't want to speak to either one of them, but at least Stevie doing ghoul or Jake Miller doing his hand-wringing-followed-by-a-warning routine would take her mind off her disquieting thoughts.

She put down the stirring spoon once again, but this time she turned off the stove before heading off to answer the phone.

Her caller was Jake Miller; he had an earful for her. Tom came home while she was in the midst of trying to calm her client. Her side of the exchange was agitated enough that Tom stopped at the office door and listened.

"I'm sorry you feel that way, Mr. Miller, but I didn't hire them and I didn't know they were going to be working in the woods today." Jake Miller's voice was so loud, Tom could hear the anger in it, if not his specific words, from where he stood.

"Of course you can fire me, but I'll still be representing Stevie, so you can't get rid of me altogether."

Tom caught Regan's eye. He was solicitous; she rolled her eyes and pantomimed a hangman holding a noose around her neck. "No, I haven't spoken to him. You need to be prepared for him to go forward with the purchase, though."

She winced. "Mr. Miller … Mr. Miller …" Regan gave up trying to speak and sat in silent acceptance of the tirade fired at her. Tom was her only comfort. He put his hands on her shoulders and began massaging them, trying to ease the tension he felt in her body.

Once his anger was spent, Jake Miller's tone changed. "No. No, you don't need to apologize. These are difficult times for everyone. Yes. Yes, considering, that's probably appropriate. I'll let him know."

"That's a new posture for Jake Miller," Regan said as she hung up. "Usually he's full of concern about how his brother doesn't want the house sold, but today he's so eager for Stevie to close the sale that he's directing his lawyer to move escrow along as quickly as possible."

"From what I overheard, Jake Miller can get pretty darned angry."

"Well, yes, that's true, too. He didn't mince words telling me how furious he is with me for not stopping the tree cutting that I didn't know was coming. Eventually, though, he did apologize for handing me my head, although I doubt his sincerity. But there were no more dire warnings about the wrath of John Miller, so I guess I'm safe in my bed tonight," she turned her head and leaned her cheek against Tom's hand, "especially with you there to protect me."

"Regan, it's Arlene," her favorite escrow officer said in a voice so soft it sounded like she was trying to keep from being overheard. "Jake Miller is in the conference room with his attorney. He came in without an appointment and his attorney insisted I get his paperwork together immediately. I asked him if we should wait for you, but he said you weren't coming. I'm printing docs now. You always come to signoffs, so if you want to come, I'll dawdle."

"No. Don't. I'm persona non grata with Jake Miller; he didn't tell me escrow was moving so quickly or that he was coming in to sign his docs; he mustn't want me there. You said he's got his highly paid attorney with him?"

"That's right."

"Good. His smarmy legal advisor can look over the paperwork on his behalf."

"What about Steven Butler's signoff?"

"Stevie's signoff?"

"He's due in at 4:30. Because we had, uh, those, uh, complications since he signed off before, he needs to sign a couple of updated documents. Do you want to be here for that?"

"No, I'll pass ... no ... yes, I'll be there."

Regan imagined Jake Miller's attorney questioning her on the witness stand. "Mrs. McHenry, isn't it true you declined to use your experienced eye to look for irregularities and errors on behalf of Mr. Miller, but did so for Mr. Butler in yet another egregious act of favoring one man over another during the supposed fair and equal representation you provided for both of your clients?"

Regan looked at the clock. If she hurried, she had just enough time to stop by one of the tasting rooms on Swift Street to buy Stevie a celebratory bottle of wine. She grabbed her purse and rushed out the office back door to the parking lot, wondering if she trusted her judgment in selecting a red for him or if she should go with an untried white. In the end, she opted for a Zinfandel from tiny Sones Cellars.

Stevie was pleased with her choice. "I haven't made it to this tasting room yet, but it was on my list. Thank you."

"We have just a few new documents for you to sign today," Arlene said as she plopped an inch-thick stack of papers on the table, "and a couple of repeats from last time. Most we don't need to go over; you just need to 'SCH' them again," she referred to Stevie's initials, "and add today's date. Here's the fun one: your deed. You need to sign right here, oh, and be sure to spell out your full name like I typed it, Steven Commons Butler, no initials allowed." Arlene pointed to the line above Stevie's typed name.

"Commons?" Regan looked at Stevie questioningly.

"Yeah." He cast a sideways glance at her so he could see her reaction. "Like the first realtor who was killed. According to my mother, Josh may have been my half-brother," he said nonchalantly. "I told you I liked to look up degrees of separation. It's interesting what you find."

"Roger Commons was your father?" Regan was incredulous.

"I was little when he was murdered. My mom remarried and my stepdad adopted me, so I have a different last name now.

"Deed's all signed," he said cheerily, pushing the deed back to Arlene. Experienced as she was, the escrow officer remained nonplussed at the mention of murder, but her discrete fleeting look at Regan hinted she expected a phone call later.

"I'd like to taste my wine now. Regan, do you want some? How about you?" he offered to Arlene. "Can we taste it while I initial stuff? Can you get us three glasses?"

"I'll see what I can find." With one more circumspect glance at Regan, Arlene headed for the door.

"Coffee mugs are okay if you don't have glasses, but no paper cups," Stevie called after her.

"Stevie, buying this house …"

"Isn't a coincidence," he smiled unperturbedly, "I do want to make wine and it's a great property for what I want to do, but if the house wasn't for sale soon, I'd have gone to Josh directly. He needed money and I wanted the house. We'd have worked something out."

"Did Josh know … about you two maybe being … ?"

"No. At least I don't think so. My full name was on the old deed I signed, printed out like it was on this one, but Josh hadn't signed any papers yet. I was going to tell him when I called the day he was killed, but the words wouldn't come out; the time wasn't right and I wanted to tell him in person, not over the phone anyway. I figured he'd call me after he saw the deed, and if he didn't, well, that meant he wasn't ready to talk about it. I could wait for another time."

Stevie let out a wicked little laugh. "I wish I could have seen Josh's uncle's face today when he saw the deed with my name on it. He thinks his brother killed Josh because he sold the house. How's old John Miller going to feel when he figures out who owns the house now?"

"It's possible Jake Miller's concern is valid. You know I was attacked at the property last week. It could have been his brother."

"Or the ghost," he chuckled.

"What are you planning to do, Stevie? You could be placing yourself at risk."

"I don't know yet." His answer was indecisive but his eyes narrowed and seemed shifty behind his huge glasses. He avoided looking at Regan. His baby-sized teeth were visible for the briefest of moments before the tip of his tongue appeared on his lips and erased the smile that revealed them. "Maybe do battle with the man who killed my father."

"Stevie, you're not playing one of your video games. What's been happening is real and dangerous; four people are dead."

He shook his head slowly, "Everything's part of the

game."

🏠🏠🏠🏠🏠🏠🏠🏠🏠🏠🏠

Dave barreled past Amanda, leaving the poor receptionist calling after him, "Dave? May I help you?"

He was a familiar enough face at Kiley and Associates that she wasn't troubled by his behavior, but she felt it was her job to announce him and she couldn't because she didn't know whether he was aimed at Regan's office or Tom's office.

He held up his hand and, without breaking stride or turning to face her, gave her a dismissive wave over his shoulder.

"Regan, you gotta reign in that Butler kid!" Dave proclaimed as he swung into her office and dropped into a chair across from her desk. He leaned toward her, not for intimacy, but for emphasis. "You're not going to believe what your little ghoul is lobbying for now."

"Hello to you, too."

Dave overlooked her satirical greeting and sputtered on at full tilt. "He wants to borrow 'his skeleton,'" Dave signaled quotation marks with fingers on either side of his face — "that's what he's calling the Vic unearthed in the woods by his new house, the house *you* sold him. He's got some cockamamie idea about having some art students at UCSC cast the skull in plaster and play with clay to make a mock-up of what the guy in the ground looked like before he went in the dirt. He says he wants to find out who the corpse is and name a wine after him.

"He's willing to make a nice donation to UCSC to fund a bunch of art students for an independent studies class, so the chancellor is happy and the Art Department is happy, and he's gonna give the Police Department a bequest for DNA testing — those things still aren't cheap, $500 a pop for court worthy tests — so the Chief's happy and willing to let him do it.

"I'm supposed to hold a press conference with that publicity hungry little weirdo, pat him on the back, and say nice things about him. Your Butler guy gives me the creeps. I don't want to make nice with him, especially when he's using a murdered man as a way to get publicity for his wine. I can't get me out of this little media event, so you've gotta talk Butler out of doing it!"

Regan was close to giggling, but she fought hard to seem calmly befuddled; she was usually the perturbed one asking for Dave's help with some intrigue she had in mind, and she didn't want to interrupt her enjoyment of their reversed roles.

"But Dave, what Stevie wants to do sounds generous and helpful. Don't the police have facial reconstructions done sometimes to help identify skeletal remains? I don't understand why you aren't pleased," she said with all the naivety she could fake.

"By the way, I assume Stevie's offer means you were mistaken about the skeleton in the woods belonging to the drug murder victim? That's a shame; you seemed pretty sure that's who the skeleton was ..." she trailed off innocently.

"That's right."

"Well then, since you didn't fill me in as promised, does this mean I don't owe you one after all?" Regan produced a smile big enough for a movie starlet's head shot.

"I don't ask for favors very often," Dave said before he lapsed into stony silence.

Regan dropped all hint of teasing. "No, you don't. I'll talk to him … but I don't have any control over him; it probably won't do any good. If you do have to work with him, try to remind yourself that Stevie, like fine wine, is an acquired taste … and that he's grown up with his own challenges. I was going to mention it the next time I saw you; I'm concerned about him, and I don't mean vis-à-vis him getting publicity for his wine."

"You mean your little ghoul is up to nastier things than figuring out how to use gore and blood as marketing tools?"

"This whole wine thing is, to some degree, a cover. His father was Roger Commons, the first realtor killed at the house. Stevie wants to catch whoever killed his father, and I'm afraid he'll put himself at risk to do it. My little ghoul, as you like to call him, may need his own guardian angel."

Dave leaned back in his seat, squeezed his eyes shut, and squirmed with displeasure. "Aw, Regan, why do you get involved with the people you do? Why didn't you cut that kid loose as soon as you knew who he was? I bet you're gonna volunteer to be that angel, too, aren't you?"

"Stevie only told me about his father at his signoff when I saw his middle name was Commons, like the murdered realtor. I didn't know who he was until late yesterday."

Dave shook his head, "Of course you didn't."

"Don't worry about me — I'm not getting involved with this one — but I think he's in need of someone, the police or someone in the Sheriff's Department maybe, to keep an eye

84

on him until John Miller is apprehended.

"I'll talk to Stevie, see if I have any sway with him, and try to get you off the publicity hook. In exchange, couldn't you use your influence to get the police to check in on him every once in a while? You might just catch Miller sooner that way. Seems like a win-win to me."

Regan could almost see the wheels turning in Dave's head as he debated whether to keep his mouth closed or tell her what the police were planning to do. Informing her won.

"We're gonna do just that. You keep asking and I keep dodging ... You win. I admit it; we do think it's likely all four murders were committed by the same person. We think it's possible the skeleton in the woods was Miller's work, too. Jake Miller has everyone in a dither about his brother being back and killing again. From what he says, it's possible the Butler kid could be on his brother's hit list, so he'll be getting some low profile protection."

🏠🏠🏠🏠🏠🏠🏠🏠🏠🏠🏠

Regan tried to reach Stevie all afternoon, leaving message after message for him. Was he screening or engrossed? She had a brief moment of panic — suppose something had already happened to him? She resorted to texting, a means of communicating she hated, spelling out her vexation: *Pick up your phone.*

His one-word reply appeared instantaneously. *Sup?*

Verbal communication call now, she thumbed.

Her phone rang immediately. Stevie said, "I like texting

better than talking."

"I don't."

"You sound like my mother."

"If I do, then I'm sure she's a sane and wonderful person."

"She is, except when someone pushes her buttons and she losses it."

Regan had a mental image of Stevie with his finger on a big red button ... she wasn't sure if it was his mother's, or Dave's, or hers.

"I understand from a friend that you have become a great benefactor to some of our local institutions."

"You mean my promised hand-outs to UCSC and the cops?"

"Uh-huh."

Stevie's chortle sounded like a series of rapid fire hiccoughs. "My contributions are a business decision. I want to know who the dead man in my trees is, or was. My neighbors told me they've still seen the ghost in the upstairs window, but haven't seen the ghost in the woods since the body was taken away. How cool is that, I mean that they've seen the woman ghost?

"I figured if I threw a little cash around, maybe I could find out who the skeleton and maybe the woodland ghost were, make Jake Miller crazy — no particular reason to do that, I guess, but it's fun and really easy to do — and maybe flush out John Miller, all while getting some major publicity for my wine. I'm getting a lot for my donation money."

"I don't like the John Miller part. I'm going to worry about ..."

"Oh, now you sound *exactly* like my mother."

"I didn't call to mother you, Stevie. I called because my friend, Dave Everett, the Santa Cruz police ombudsman you'll be holding your news conference with, asked me to. He's a good friend; I said I would. He wants you to skip the media …"

"He wants me to be a secret donor?"

"Let's say a quiet donor, one who doesn't stand in front of a bunch of cameras with a UCSC rep and Dave as the police representative flanking him."

"I don't think so. I want to get massive publicity with my announcement. I'm going to tell the world who my real father was and do all sorts of things that will make John Miller unhappy and give a date when it's going to happen. He'll have a deadline if he wants to stop me. He'll have to try, at least I hope so. I need the word to be out, big time, to be sure he hears my plans. Tell your friend to deal with it."

Regan was surprised how readily Tom agreed to come along with her to Stevie's media event.

"I have to see this owlish person who's managed to get Dave so worked up. It should be an interesting day. I'll drive."

They were early, but cars already lined the driveway and spilled into the street in front of the Murder House. A young man dressed haphazardly in clothing that wasn't intended to be worn together was positioned at the base of the drive. He waved his arms to stop each arriving car and nervously checked his phone when each driver told him his name. His job seemed to be making sure only official media vehicles and people whose names were on a list on his smart phone were allowed to drive up and park near the house.

"This is quite a turnout." Tom swung his car out of the check-in cue. "Let's skip the interview," he remarked as he pulled down the road to park. "In addition to his other skills, your client seems to have a talent for generating a crowd."

When they walked to the top of the driveway, they passed by a wooden sign suspended above the front lawn on tall posts which read *Welcome to Murder House Wines*. It was festooned with purple balloons that resembled clusters of oversized grapes.

"I guess Stevie's decided on his winery's name," Regan snickered. "He likes to shock people."

"Then his choice is a good one. That name ought to raise a few eyebrows. Do you think it will sell wine, though?" Tom wondered.

Elegant refreshments and glasses of champagne were set out on tables scattered across the lawn that separated the driveway from the steps leading up to the house. Among the various guests nibbling on the fare were many local winemakers, recognizable as such because they sported tee-shirts emblazoned with their winery logos. Regan bet it was Stevie's idea to tell the vintners that, if they came, they could promote their wineries. It ensured a good turnout; free publicity for a commercial venture was rarely declined.

Tom, who was much better than she was at remembering faces, recognized several mid-to-high level UCSC administrators, local officials, businessmen, and politicians he had met at Shakespeare/Santa Cruz events and pointed them out to her.

"Stevie's donation must be sizable to draw so many dignitaries," Regan observed, "but not obscenely so, because the Chancellor and the Chief of Police are notably absent. Oh, there's Dave; doesn't he look morose? Shall we go try to cheer him up?"

Regan waved to Dave when she caught his eye. He gave her a dour smirk in return and began moving through the crowd in their direction, but Stevie appeared in front of them

89

from out of the milieu before Dave reached them, and their friend turned away to avoid him.

"Regan, this is so cool. Everybody came." Stevie's normally pasty skin glowed and his cheeks were flushed with bright pink spots that betrayed his excitement. "My mom and dad are here; even Josh's Uncle Jake showed up." He pushed his glasses up the bridge of his nose and went up on tip-toes so he could whisper in Regan's ear, cupping his hand against her head for privacy.

"There's going to be a special event. I want you to know so you don't freak when things start happening. Go stand over by where the trees were taken down for the best view," he whispered. He gave her a quick baby-teeth revealing smile and flitted away before she could ask what he meant.

"He's your little owl?" Tom asked.

"He is."

"I see why you call him that."

Regan took Tom's hand and tugged him in the direction of the cleared trees. "He just gave me a heads-up. I think he's about to outdo himself. He says we should be over here to best take in his show."

At some unknown signal that had been orchestrated ahead of time, participants in the media event began coalescing around Stevie. Vintners formed a semicircle behind him on the top of the first stair landing. The UCSC representative stood to his right, down one step, and Dave, resplendent in his brightest Hawaiian shirt, and also down one step, stood to his left. The clever arrangement not only made Stevie the center of focus, it made him seem taller and more imposing than he was. Regan was sure Stevie's careful planning went into making him appear so prominent.

Dave held a hand mic and called for quiet. Regan could only imagine how thrilled he must be to be the master of ceremonies and how disappointed he was that she hadn't saved him from having to fulfill the media relations part of his job description.

Cameras rolled. Dave introduced the head of the UCSC Art Department and Stevie, whom he thanked on behalf of the Police Department for his offer to fund one-hundred DNA tests. There was polite applause as Dave handed the mic to the UCSC representative, who also thanked Stevie and explained how twelve students had already signed up for the independent studies class he was funding.

More applause followed before Stevie took the mic. "Thank you all for coming today. I have a couple of announcements to make." Stevie was surprisingly poised as he spoke, "I will be making my donations in five days' time. The Santa Cruz Police Department has made a plaster cast of the murdered man's skull found in my woods right over there," he swept his hand in the direction of where Tom and Regan and several other people were standing, "and the students in the class I'm funding will use it to create a facial reconstruction model of the victim's face. The first of my hundred DNA tests will be done on my man's bones. I hope with that combined information, he'll be identified. I want to know who he was so I can name the first release of my Murder House Sangiovese after him."

There were a few gasps in the audience and murmured words before Stevie continued, "I want to make my wine here because I have a special tie to this house." His voice rose to a higher pitch and shook with emotion, "My father was Roger Commons. He was murdered here almost twenty years ago." The buzz from the audience grew louder. Stevie shouted into the mic, high color spreading over more of his face, "John Miller, you murderer, I'm serving you notice. I'm taking your house. Your house! Unless you stop me now, your wife's ghost will belong to me!" Stevie raised his free hand in a clenched fist as he finished his challenge.

A series of sharp reports sounded from near the front of the house. Purple grape-balloons on the *Murder House Wines* sign exploded. There were a few startled screams from the spectators. The media crews spun their cameras around wildly, trying to capture what was happening. Forewarned as she was, Regan kept her eyes on Stevie. The baby-teethed grin on his face looked triumphant … and predatory.

A single explosive sound, different from the ones they heard seconds before, echoed across the assembled crowd, not from in front of the house, though, but from the direction of the woods behind where Regan and Tom stood.

Several vintners hit the deck as blood exploding in a red froth from the Art Director's shoulder spattered them. Dave tackled a still exhilarated Stevie, forced him to the ground, and covered him with his body.

In the stunned silence that followed the single gunshot, Dave was on his feet again, brandishing a service revolver produced from under his Hawaiian shirt. He charged down the steps and pushed through the congregation of bystanders, dodging those who crouched on the ground like a football player practices high stepping through tires. Then he ran across the lawn in front of where Tom and Regan stood and charged past Tom on his way toward the woods.

Tom held his hand up to his ear and shook his head. When he removed his hand, it was bloody.

"Tom!" Regan screamed, "You're bleeding!" She pressed her hand to the side of his face. "You're hurt!" She threw her arms around him and hugged him to her, but no matter how tightly she held her husband, it felt like she couldn't hold him closely enough.

A bystander peeled off his tee-shirt and thrust it at Tom, instructing him to wad it up and use it to keep pressure on his wound. The man rushed off bare-chested in the direction of the fallen Art Department head, who was swarmed by people either trying to help him or trying to get a better look at him.

"Let me through," the man shouted. "I can help. I was a medic in the Air Force."

Dave was back from the woods and by their side in a matter of moments. "You okay, pal?" he put a hand on Tom's shoulder and watched his face closely as Tom answered, looking for signs that Tom was injured more seriously than he seemed to be.

"I'm fine. I heard a rush of air and felt a sting; I thought Bonny Doon's biggest mosquito had just taken a bite out of me. I'm only nicked."

"Good," Dave said. "Do me a favor then. Stay right where you are until someone marks your position. Your misfortune could save us a lot of time trying to figure out where the shooter was. If we place you on the bullet trajectory line — we should be able to backtrack into the woods and pinpoint where the bullet was fired from. That'll help us scare up some evidence, maybe figure out who the shooter was."

Tom gently reassured his wife, "I'm fine, sweetheart, really, I'm fine. Let go of me before I get blood on you."

Regan began slowly relinquishing her hold on him. As she did, she began shaking, not with fear, but with rage. "Let's ask Stevie who it was. He said he had a special event planned; this must have been it."

"He what?" Dave's face contorted with anger. "This is his doing? Someone could have been killed. I'd like to rip that publicity grubbing irresponsible brat apart with my bare hands."

Regan brushed Tom's cheek with a kiss. "You're sure you're okay?"

"Positive."

"Then I'm going to go help Dave kill my client," she stated matter-of-factly.

They set off toward the center of the maelstrom at the first stair landing. Dave yelled, "Police! Let me pass," and didn't hesitate to pitch slow moving bystanders out of his way as he forced his way through the crowd. Regan followed in his wake.

Stevie was sitting on the spot where he had stood to deliver his ultimatum to John Miller. He was pale again but still smiling, although his grin looked fixed and was without expression or excitement.

"On your feet, Butler. Hands behind your back," Dave commanded.

"What?" Stevie's question was more of a whimper than a query. His only response to Dave's directive was to cringe and shrink lower.

Dave grabbed Stevie's arm and pulled him to his feet.

94

"I'm arresting you for conspiracy to do great bodily harm. Be glad I'm not arresting you for attempted murder."

Dave was all business and in professional control as he produced a piece of plastic, the latest lightweight police handcuffs, from the arsenal of equipment he kept under his Hawaiian shirt, and encircled Stevie's wrists. "You have the right to remain silent ..." Dave began his Mirandizing drone.

Regan was not in any way calm or controlled. "This is your idea of a special event? What's wrong with you?" she demanded.

"I didn't do this. Not this! Look at me. I have blood on me. I could have been killed. All I did was wire the balloons with firecrackers so my friend could explode them on cue."

A petite woman with hair worn long and as white-blonde as Stevie's struggled through the crowd. "Stevie, Stevie," she called out as she came. The crowd refused to part for her as it had for Dave; she was red-faced and glistening with perspiration by the time she reached the handcuffed Stevie.

"What are you doing?" she shrieked at Dave, giving him an ineffective shove as she rebuked him. "Take your hands off my son, you bully. He has a weak heart; he's doesn't need you manhandling him. Sweetie, are you hurt?" she quizzed Stevie.

"No, Mom."

If Stevie had any adrenaline left in him, it dissipated in his mother's presence. He was barely responsive when Jake Miller burst onto the scene. "Now you've done it, you stupid boy," he hissed. "You couldn't just quietly buy the house — oh no — you had to taunt him; you had to go out of your way to make my brother angry. Angrier. Back off. Drop this class

95

thing and this DNA thing, and this trying to find out who the man in the woods was for your wine label and publicity stunts. My brother was a marksman when he was in the army. Consider what he did here as just a warning shot. The next time he comes after you, I promise you, he won't miss."

The ambulance took the wounded Art Director away, and Stevie was put in the back of a police cruiser and hauled away for questioning. A girl who was newly hired in the crime scene unit was assigned the menial task of placing a stake to indicate Tom's location and the height of his wounded ear. She finished pounding the stake into the ground where he stood, and Tom was free to go.

"Should we take you to urgent care? You may need a stitch or two," Regan asked.

"I'd rather go to a jewelry store," Tom grinned. "As long as I have a hole in my ear, this may be the right time to buy a diamond stud and have my ear pierced. Getting my ear pierced must be on my bucket list somewhere."

"It's your right ear that's hurt. My understanding is that straight men pierce their left ear," Regan teased in keeping with Tom's jest. "It's up to you, though."

"Okay. Urgent care, then."

Tom noticed what a distracted driver his wife was as she negotiated Highway 1 from Bonny Doon Road toward the Westside Urgent Care Clinic. "You're awfully quiet. I'm fine, you know. You're only driving because I don't want to take pressure off my ear and risk getting blood in my car."

"Hmm? I know. I was thinking."

"About?"

"About whether or not Stevie could have been behind today's shooting. Dave thinks he was."

"And your conclusion?"

"I don't think so. Stevie is self-absorbed and publicity hungry, but I don't think he'd put people at risk. He was trying to provoke John Miller with today's show — the attack must mean he succeeded — Miller must have been the assailant." She ended her statement not with finality but with a note of perplexity, "But if the shooter was John Miller, a man who has already committed murder, and who according to his brother is a marksman, I wonder why he didn't kill Stevie?"

"That's an excellent question," Tom replied.

10

No progress had been made in catching the Murder House Winery event shooter when Stevie called Regan four weeks later.

"I'm having another event tomorrow. It's private. No media. You and your husband can come if you want, but you can't bring your cop friend. I don't like him."

"That's fair. Dave doesn't like you, either. He still thinks you set up the shooting at your last event. Tom's ear has healed well — thanks for asking. Your mother sent him a nice get-well-soon card on your behalf, by the way; please thank her for me the next time you talk to her. What's your event this time?"

"Most of the students in my class have finished their facial reconstructions. I'm gonna set up bases with a reconstructed head on each one in a circle around where my bones were found. We'll unveil the busts one at a time; it should be exciting."

"I'm surprised you don't want to drag a few reporters to the unveiling."

"I thought about it, but I'd rather wait to see how good the faces look. The students are talented sculptors generally, but I don't know if they're any good at doing facial reconstruction, which is kind of subjective anyway.

"I passed out the skull casts to the students at my house. We did it in the cleared woods where my skeleton was found so they could kind of pick up a vibe of who the dead man was. Then we got drunk and stoned out our minds. We'll see if it worked.

"My mother and dad are going to be here tomorrow. If you come by, you can thank Mom for the card yourself. Oh, and I hired security guards, so it's safe."

"Then how can I resist coming?"

Unlike last time, Tom was reluctant to attend Stevie's event. He rubbed his ear absentmindedly the whole time he tried to talk Regan out of going but, in the end, he agreed to go with her.

"I don't like this one bit," he said as he walked with Regan to the parking area behind their office when it was time to leave for the Murder House. "It's not too late to change your mind."

"You don't have to come with me. I'll be safe. Remember? Stevie says he's hired security."

"Pfff." Tom's airy disparagement made it clear what he thought of Stevie's safety measures.

"He's not using this event for publicity, either. It's going to be different from last time. You'll see."

When they reached the Murder House, they were able to drive up to the parking area in front of the house. Stevie had honored his pledge to keep the event quiet and private; there were no media vehicles to be seen. The wooden *Welcome to Murder House Wines* sign remained, but it had been moved closer to the house and was unadorned. It seemed less prominent. There were fewer tables set out than at the media event, and champagne had been replaced by wine, coconut water, and iced tea.

"Looks like Stevie is playing the day in a low-key way," Regan noted.

"The day is young," Tom said with raw cynicism. "To be fair, I have noticed stern men dressed in black scattered around the perimeter, but it's hard to know if they're there for security or because Stevie thinks they look cool. Let's keep our heads down in case it's the latter."

Regan noticed the men, too. She also noted Stevie's list-checking friend from the media event had replaced his haphazard clothing with Goth-like all black. Maybe Tom was right, and Stevie's men-in-black were more for effect than protection.

She spotted Stevie's mother wandering among the tables, picking a tidbit here and there, and loading it onto her plate. Regan squeezed Tom's hand. "I'll be right back. I see Stevie's mom. I'm going to say hello to her."

"Mrs. Butler?" Regan queried, "Thank you for sending my husband a card."

Mrs. Butler responded with a smile that was like Stevie's: tiny, precise, and filled with baby-sized teeth. "I'm sorry about what happened to him — I'm Myra, by the way. Is your husband here; was he willing to brave today after his experience?"

"He was. He came — reluctantly, though."

"Mine didn't," she chuckled.

"Was he afraid John Miller would turn up again?"

Myra Butler's eyes opened wide and she inhaled sharply. Her startled reaction was fleeting, but apparent enough that Regan couldn't miss it.

"I'm sorry," Regan stumbled, "I ... I didn't mean to upset you with the mention of that man. I'm so sorry. It must have been horrible for you, losing your first husband in the way you did; you don't need me reminding you. And you must be concerned about Stevie after all that's happened recently."

"We aren't afraid of John Miller. Will you excuse me, please?" Myra Butler turned on her heel abruptly — leaving Regan abandoned and dismissed — and hurried away, her long white-blonde hair swinging gently behind her with each step.

Stevie, also a man-in-black, stood on the first step landing and tapped his wine glass with a fork. The soft tinkling sound it made was a recognized call for attention. Regan's view of him was partly obscured by another guest. She moved to see him clearly. Stevie had a holster strapped around his middle, not down low and slanted like a steely-eyed gunslinger's in an old western, but cinched at his waist. Worn as it was, his gun looked geeky — but loaded.

"If you'll all follow me, we're gonna start. It's okay if you bring food with you."

Stevie fairly danced down the steps, smiling more openly than Regan had ever seen him smile, and led the way into the woodland clearing. Folding chairs had been set out in several short rows. "Take a seat," he motioned toward them as he proceeded to the center of ten draped stands arranged in a flattened semi-circle behind him. A single person stood behind each of the displays, presumably the artist responsible for the creation under wraps.

"Let me tell you about facial reconstruction," Stevie began in a voice loud enough to be heard all the way to the back row of seats. "First of all, rods of different lengths are inserted into models of a skull according to the best understanding an anthropologist or criminologist has come up with of what kind of person the skull might have belonged to in life.

"We know from studying his skeleton that my bones belonged to a man between thirty and forty years old, and that he was most likely Caucasian, so those were the broad guidelines used for placing the rods.

"Next, artists put fake eyes in the center of the skull sockets — my students used brown eyes because more people have brown eyes than blue eyes — and add clay to the head to simulate the muscles of the face. You have to be good at anatomy to do that," Stevie chortled in one of his little bird giggles.

"The artists use a whole series of calculations to figure out how broad noses are and how wide lips are likely to be — you can read about it on my website if you're interested — but a lot of what comes next is up to the artist.

"I can't wait any longer," Stevie hollered enthusiastically. "Let's see what they came up with. Let's meet the ghost in the woods."

He turned to watch as the first student slipped the drape off his bust. There was polite tentative applause from the onlookers before the next student in line repeated the process. Stevie indicated the timing of each of the following reveals by waving his arms in the air like a maestro conducting his orchestra.

Each bust was different, yet there was a commonality about them — and a familiarity. Regan frowned as the busts continued to be revealed. Although she couldn't quite put her finger on who it was, they reminded her of someone. As the final bust was undraped, the who became clear. The final bust incorporated features hinted at in the preceding busts, but it went beyond an aggregation of resemblance. She looked at Tom. He turned to face her and nodded.

Jake Miller. The busts reminded her of Jake Miller, the final bust could have been a sculpture of him.

"It's Uncle Jake," Tom said.

Regan tried to see Stevie's face, but he remained with his back to the seated guests so she couldn't tell if he recognized the resemblance between the busts and the former owner's uncle. When he finally did face his audience, Stevie was subdued and unsmiling.

"That concludes our …"

"Hey, Bird, your mom!" Stevie's dark-clad friend yelled.

Myra Butler lay on the ground near her empty seat in the midst of a white-blonde halo of hair. She was out cold in a dead faint.

"Dave Everett." His curt greeting meant Regan was catching him in the midst of what he considered serious work — real police work — not involved in something frivolous like handling citizen complaints about the new dog-friendly rules for the downtown — another official part of his job, when he wasn't interfacing with the media, but something he didn't enjoy.

"Have you taken a break for lunch yet?"

"No, and I'm starved."

"If you're willing to meet me and sit still for a minute, I'll buy," Regan enticed.

"I'm kinda ..." he sighed and then there was a long, silent pause on his end, "Okay. Someplace close ... and fast ... that has big servings of fried fish. I'm in the mood for greasy, and lots of it. You should know I know you're up to something, so this meal is gonna cost you. I'll want dessert, too."

"Is Gilda's on the wharf the sort of place you had in mind?"

"Add mind reading to your list of talents. See you there in twenty."

Dave slid into a chair without saying hello. He grabbed a menu, flipped it open to the fried foods section, and ran his finger down the right side, scanning prices. "Hmm, looks like the seafood platter is the priciest thing here; that'll do." His smile was big enough to contain an "I told you so." When the server took their orders, Dave added cheesecake and coffee to his request.

With ordering concluded to his satisfaction, he leaned

back in his seat and asked Regan, "How do I rate being taken to lunch? What did you do this time?"

"I didn't do anything. I'm here to give you useful information. In fact, you should be buying my lunch."

"I'll keep that in mind. Whadda-ya have for me?"

"Stevie Butler ..."

Regan didn't get out more than Stevie's name before Dave rolled his eyes and cut her off. "Not your little ghoul. It's been a month or more without a peep out of you about him; I had high hopes you'd moved on."

"Sorry," Regan shook her head. "Consider that month-long time-out an intermission, not an end of the play. Stevie called a couple of days ago and invited Tom and me to another event. There was drama — it seems there's always drama when Stevie does anything — but there were no media types there and no violence this time. He held an unveiling for the facial reconstructions the UCSC art students did."

Dave chuckled, "I'm not sorry I missed that, especially since facial recognition is so subjective and artist driven; it's generally a waste of time."

"I don't think that's true in this case."

Dave looked at her askance. "You see someone you knew?"

"That's one of the things I want to talk to you about. I think I did see someone I know."

Dave squinted his good eye ever so slightly. Uncharacteristically, his prosthetic eye didn't follow suit; he must have mastered how much movement his real eye could make without setting off the corresponding muscles of his other eye. To Regan, he looked like a wary pirate. "Who might that be?"

"The reconstructions reminded me of Josh Miller's uncle. The skeletal remains can't be him, of course, because he's alive and well, but ... do you know if Jake resembled his brother John?"

"Are you saying you think the man buried in the woods is John Miller, everyone's favorite quadruple murder suspect?"

"I think that is what I'm saying. I didn't get a lot of sleep last night — and neither did Tom because I kept waking him up to ask if he thought my theories were reasonable — but we finally agreed that the skeleton may well be Miller's, and that my ideas kind of make sense.

"No one has seen John Miller since the first murders. It was assumed he ran off after killing his wife and her lover, but maybe he didn't. I think he never went anywhere, that the real killer murdered him and buried him in the woods to make it seem like he ran off, and used his disappearance to throw everyone off the real trail."

Their smiling server, with the practiced timing of so many people in his profession, arrived with their meals in the middle of Regan's narrative. "Seafood platter for you, sir; crab salad for you, ma'am," he said as he placed heaped plates in front of them.

Neither Dave nor Regan made any attempt to begin eating; they didn't even touch their forks. Dave's elbow rested on the arm of his chair, he put his hand to his chin and silently rubbed a finger up and down over his lips.

"John Miller and his brother were born close together; I'd have to look it up, but I think John's the elder by a little more than a year. I've seen photos of them together in the Miller/

Commons murder file — pictures got trotted out and passed around after the Miller kid and your realtor friend were killed — in those pictures, I'd say Jake's the spittin' image of John.

"Maybe I've been too hard on your little weirdo. He insisted the first DNA test his grant paid for was to be done on the Vic in the woods, so it's on file. All we'll need now is some of Jake Miller's DNA and we can look for a family relationship. I bet 'ole Jake will provide that Johnny-on-the-spot; he'd love to clear his brother's name. I'll give him a call."

"That will take time, won't it? Can't you check dental records?"

"Miller's a suspect in a murder case, not a missing person. We don't get dental records for murderers unless they bite the Vic."

Regan didn't know if what Dave was saying was the beginning of one of his punch lines or the end of his statement.

"It's probably too late to get them now, even if his brother knows the name of his dentist. After this long, the dentist's probably tossed 'em; they only have to keep records for about a decade. Patience is a virtue, you know, Regan."

"If the skeleton belongs to John Miller, that changes everything, doesn't it?"

"Oooh yeah," Dave nodded for emphasis as he drew out his pronouncement. "It'd mean we start over and look at everyone surrounding the murders with fresh eyes.

"You said this Miller deal was one of the things you wanted to talk to me about." He skewered a prawn and dunked it in tartar sauce. "What else is on your mind?" he asked before popping it into his mouth.

"I have an idea — I have a theory about who might have killed him."

Their collegial exchange ended with Dave's disdainful, "Of course you do."

"I'm not going to tell you about it, though; I've changed my mind. I'll hold off sharing my theory with you until we know that the skeleton belongs to John Miller. I could be wrong about it being him, you know, and I'd hate to defame someone who doesn't deserve it."

"What? You're suddenly shy about throwing out suspects' names? When did that start?" Dave sat up stiffly in his seat and pointed his fork at Regan. "Flaming about your latest murder suspect is what you do."

"It's what I've done in the past," she agreed, "but I've learned from my mistakes. I'll wait."

"Regan, I can't let you pay for lunch," Dave's tone was almost reverential. "You gave me a decent clue to pursue, you backed off of your usual wild accusations, and you admitted you make mistakes, all in a single day. It doesn't get any better than that.

"But come on now," he wrinkled his nose, "give me a name. At least give me a hint … for your own good, so we can investigate and keep you out of trouble."

Her response was a big smile … and silence. Then she put a mouthful of crab salad into her mouth that was so large, she couldn't talk even if she wanted to.

"Wait." He flashed a knowing look. "I get it. All this talk about your ideas is as fishy as my lunch. You don't really have anybody in mind at all; you figured with me primed by grease and French fries, I'd offer you something — my idea of the next prime suspect — and you could start playing detective again. Not gonna happen, Regan. I'm onto you this time."

The idea of killing two birds with one stone appealed to Regan. She had to make a trip to the County Building anyway — her new listing in the Soquel hills meant a visit to the Environmental Health Department for copies of the well and septic permits for her client's disclosure packet — and County Records was in the same building. She could take the first step in testing her late-night theory with a visit there. If she was right, she might know in a few minutes. If she was mistaken, it could be the end of the trail for her suppositions, too.

The one car in the packed visitor parking lot with tail lights on indicating it was about to leave was only teasing. The departing driver turned on the ignition, but then, with her foot on the brake creating the tantalizing promise that she was about to back up, she didn't move. The driver studied her face in the mirror, refreshed her lipstick, rifled through her purse in search of a hairbrush, fluffed her hair, got out her cell phone and dialed, put the phone to her ear, and finally began the slow one-handed process of backing her large SUV out of its space. It took her two passes to turn sufficiently to clear the surrounding parked cars so she could go forward.

Normally Regan would have been frustrated at the driver's unhurried progress, instead she watched serenely, yawning. After her sleepless night — she should have had another cup of coffee, maybe two, during her lunch with Dave — she couldn't muster impatience. She wondered if Tom was faring any better than she was.

Their restive night had started innocently enough with them agreeing that if the skeletal remains in the woods belonged to John Miller, then he obviously couldn't have committed the Murder House's two recent killings, and if his remains found their way to an unmarked grave at about the same time as the first murders, he hadn't killed his wife and Roger Commons, either.

That was as far as their reasoned discussion had gone before another idea popped into their heads, and they went to bed, if not to sleep, early.

But Regan fell asleep wondering — if not John Miller — who was responsible for what happened at the Murder House; who had a reason for killing the first three victims. By a little after midnight, Regan drifted in the realm between sleep and wakefulness. An apparition surrounded by swirling white mist chased her in the Murder House woods, screeching unintelligibly. She ran, but the heels on her shoes were mired in the forest floor. The specter cornered her at the edge of a precipice. She spun away and tried to run in another direction, but she wasn't fast enough to escape. The ghostly creature caught hold of her and tugged at her midsection, trying to pull her backwards toward him. Her heart pounded as she struggled to wake up and escape the specter's clutches.

When she opened her eyes, she realized that Cinco, their little female cat, was standing on her stomach to gain a better vantage point, clawing at her blanket, and bawling in a deep guttural meow at something outside. Harry, their big gray cat, hurled himself against the sliding door in their bedroom. The night was cloudless, the moon was a day from being full — she could have read by its light — she didn't have to strain to see the fox strutting on the low brick wall that edged their patio, taunting the cats.

The cheeky fox never stayed near their house for more than a few days, but he was a regular who turned up several times a year to reassure himself that his mojo still worked, that he could still get a rise out of Cinco and Harry, and that he could still get them to wake their mistress in the middle of the night. Satisfied that he remained the master trickster, he disappeared over the patio wall.

Cinco returned to her foot-of-the-bed post, purring contentedly and taking full credit for chasing him away; she was asleep within a minute. Harry continued to pace by the window, remaining vigilant in case the fox was using his disappearance as a dodge while getting ready for a second confrontation farther along the wall.

Regan was glad to have been awakened; she still trembled from her too-real nightmare. Even fully awake, she could see the face of the ghostly presence from her dream: it belonged to Jake Miller, the surrogate face for his brother. She had made him one of the Murder House ghosts, the light in the woods — understandable given yesterday's revelations — but there was something about the creature she created in her troubled dream that reminded her of someone else, too.

She squeezed her eyes shut, trying to see the rest of her ghost once more. The swirling white vapor that surrounded Jake Miller's face became less ethereal and more substantive: it became Myra Butler's long white-blonde hair swinging loosely like it had when she turned tail and snubbed Regan at Stevie's unveiling party.

Regan hadn't meant to be cruel; she wished she hadn't brought up John Miller the moment his name left her mouth. Her indelicate suggestion that he might turn up again, like he did at Stevie's last event, had upset Myra; she was sure of it.

But Myra hadn't fainted then. In fact, she said she wasn't afraid of John Miller, and she should have been; wasn't he the man who killed her husband and took a shot at her son? Instead Myra fainted at the conclusion of the facial reconstruction unveilings, and Regan was certain the woman's collapse wasn't because of a delayed reaction to her foot-in-the-mouth comment.

To the crowd of concerned people patting Myra's hand, getting her water, and in every way they could think of aiding her, Myra said she was fine and blamed her fainting spell on heat exhaustion. She said she had expected cool June fog in the lower Bonny Doon Road area and had worn clothing that was too warm for what turned out to be a sunny day. The day was warm, Regan would give her that, but comfortably so, only in the low seventies.

Myra fainted as the final facial reconstruction was unveiled. The timing of her free-fall gave Regan pause. It seemed like Jake Miller's likeness in the bust had something to do with Myra's spell. As the murder victim's wife, Myra must have seen photos of John Miller or at least followed the newspaper's account and seen pictures of him there. Had Myra, like she and Tom, recognized Jake and thought of John?

Myra said she didn't fear John Miller — Regan thought that was an audacious statement. But perhaps Myra wasn't being as brash as she initially thought. Questions had huddled in the back of her mind all day — tonight they made her dream of Myra — now she asked them. Was Myra unafraid of him because she knew John Miller was dead? Did she know because she was there when his body went into the ground? Was she fearful others would realize who was buried in the woods and reconsider who was responsible for the Murder House deaths?

Regan closed her eyes tightly and rolled her head back and forth on her pillow. *Go back to sleep. The way you can put things together; you can come up with the most bizarre connections in the middle of the night.*

A memory challenged her quick repudiation. She recalled the comment that Jackie Donahue made about Roger Commons on the way to Inez's memorial: *"I don't know how his wife put up with him; I'd have killed him if I were her".*

The ideas Regan came up with in the wee hours were often farfetched, but they weren't always wrong. In the eerie blue moonlight flooding her bedroom, she began to wonder if the petite woman with ghostly white-blonde hair was capable of doing what Jackie suggested.

Stevie's mother might have reached her breaking point because of her husband's womanizing. She might have murdered her husband and his mistress and then killed John Miller and buried his body so he would seem like a runaway killer.

Myra Butler as the murderer of three people was a huge leap to make. And if John Miller was dead and didn't kill Josh and Inez, Myra must have murdered them as well. Five people. Could Myra Butler possibly have the blood of five people on her hands? Did Myra Butler as a murderer make any sense at all?

"Tom? Tom, are you awake?" she asked, even though she could hear that his breathing was regular and heavy, a borderline snore and a clear indication that he wasn't.

Regan put her hand on his arm and shook him gently. "Tom?"

"Umm. What?"

"I've been thinking … I wonder … if maybe Myra Butler killed John Miller."

His voice was thick with sleep, "That's nice."

"Tom, really."

"Uh-huh."

"I think maybe she killed her husband … and the Miller woman … and John Miller … and buried him in the woods so it would look like he was the murderer, and that he ran away …"

"Could we talk about this in the morning?" Tom turned on his side with his back to his wife and pulled the blanket up to his ear.

Regan lay on her back, rigid, her hands balled into fists. She couldn't fall back asleep. Not now.

Apparently Tom couldn't either. In a couple of minutes, he threw back the blanket and turned to face her, unhappily wide awake.

"I don't think it's possible, but for the sake of argument — and I'm only throwing this out right now so we can get some sleep — assume you're right and that Stevie's mother is the Murder House's ..." he faltered in search of the right word, "murderess from all those years ago.

"How'd she manage to do it? Let's say she somehow surprised her husband at the Miller's house — and for starters, you do see what a quandary her confronting him there creates, don't you — and bashed him over the head. If she knocked him out, I guess she could have finished him off at her leisure. But what about the Millers? How could she have done them in? See. It doesn't work."

He resumed his cozy position. "So goodnight, sweetheart."

Regan lay still and imagined. Perhaps Myra confronted Mrs. Miller first. She might have wanted to believe her husband was only a weak, susceptible fool, and that the Miller woman was the seducer in their relationship. Myra might have met with her and asked her to leave Roger alone. Regan could picture Myra pleading with the Miller woman, *"Please, for the sake of my little boy, don't break up our marriage."*

Regan set her scene in the Miller kitchen, with the two women initially talking civilly over a cup of coffee. Her thoughts came more and more rapidly; she was on a roll. Perhaps Mrs. Miller laughed at her pleadings and, in a rage, Myra seized a knife from an angled butcher block holder on the counter — there probably was one, they were all the rage about twenty years ago — and chased the adulteress upstairs where a struggle ensued.

"Tom? Tom, Myra could have killed the Miller woman

116

first. And then Roger ..."

"Tomorrow. Please," he said without moving.

Regan didn't speak, but Tom could feel her agitation.

He flipped on his back and held his hands up in a gesture of exasperation. "I've got an early meeting with some other brokers. We're going to discuss a promotional campaign aimed at getting Silicon Valley people to buy in Santa Cruz County." He dropped his arms to his sides and sighed his defeat.

"Okay. She killed the Miller woman and then her husband. What about John Miller? Little woman like her; how did she manage to kill Miller and get him in the ground?" Tom folded his hands on his chest.

"Dream up an answer for that. Goodnight, Regan."

Regan started over. Josh Miller had described seeing his father covered with blood. Could John Miller have happened upon Myra — no — could he have found his blood-soaked wife, embraced her lifeless body, and then staggered back downstairs in shock, where he was attacked by Myra ...

"Tom, I have one more question ..."

Tom sat upright in bed. "I'm not getting any sleep until we hash this out, am I?"

Regan smiled feebly, wondering if he could see her face clearly in the moonlight. He understood her so well; she was a lucky woman: he stilled loved her in spite of it.

"I'm afraid not."

Tom exhaled noisily, "Okay. What?"

"I can still imagine Myra meeting with the Miller woman and asking her to end the affair. When she said no, I can still see an incensed Myra grabbing a kitchen knife, chasing Mrs.

Miller upstairs, and attacking her in a crime of passion. Now suppose John Miller came home right after Myra killed Mrs. Miller, found his wife dead, and got her blood on him in the process."

Tom yawned. "I do remember you saying Josh Miller saw his father at the murder scene."

"That's right. He said his father had so much blood on him that he was hard to recognize. Myra could have still been in the house hiding somewhere. After Josh saw his dad, Myra could have come out, slipped up on him, and attacked him from behind. She might have been able to bring him down with a well-placed stab. Couldn't she have finished him off when he couldn't fight back like you suggested she could have done with her husband?"

"I didn't suggest," Tom protested. "I acquiesced."

He scratched his head. "I see two problems looming. First, if Myra killed Miller the way you describe, his blood would have been everywhere. But his blood mustn't have been present — at least not more than could be explained by his wife scratching him or by the realtor landing a blow in a fight for his life — or he would have been thought of as another victim instead of as the prime suspect.

"The second problem with your scenario is: how did Myra get John Miller's dead body out of the house and into a grave in the woods without dragging him there — something I'd question that she could do alone anyway — without leaving an obvious trail? Remember what happened with Inez? The police would have noticed evidence like that."

Regan rolled her eyes around like she might see answers if she looked in the right direction. "I don't know. It's the middle of the night and I'm not up to thinking clearly."

"Exactly. Can we finish this discussion in the morning when we're both clear-headed and rested?"

Regan suddenly hit on a plausible-for-the-middle-of-the-night answer for the second of Tom's problems. "Before you go back to sleep, I have another idea. Maybe she didn't stab him. Maybe she clobbered him with ... with, how about a frying pan in keeping with my kitchen weapons theme? A big heavy cast iron skillet," she laughed at her own expense. "Anyway, let's say Myra hit him with something that she could have taken away from the scene. There might not have been much blood."

"At this hour of the night, I'll agree. There might not have been much blood," Tom said in a tired monotone. "Are we done, yet?"

"Probably. I'll let you go back to sleep. Goodnight."

They lay next to one another silently.

"I'm going to regret asking, I know, but you still haven't gotten Miller to his grave. How'd Myra Butler do that? And what about her dead husband? When did he come into your murder scene? Hmm?"

"Don't know," Regan shrugged, pushing her shoulders into her pillow, "I'll have to think about it some more."

"Alone, please. Or with Harry. Or tomorrow morning. In any way you want, or with any one you want, as long as it isn't with me tonight." He threw himself onto his side and pulled the blankets up again.

Regan waited until Tom's breathing told her he had fallen asleep again before she climbed out of bed, put on her robe, and softly called to Harry, who followed her invitation doggishly, and went with her to the living room.

By the time Harry was settled on her lap, splayed on his back with his feet in the air so she could scratch his stomach, Regan knew Tom was right: Myra would have needed help disposing of John Miller's body. She ran one scene in her mind that involved a highly skilled and manipulative Myra killing the Miller woman first, and then John Miller, and finally her husband — who arrived after her rampage — right after she convinced him to help her with the woodland burial and after luring him back to the Murder House foyer to meet his fate.

Regan played with language the murderess might have used on Roger Commons to win his compliance, but everything she imagined Myra saying to him implied he was stupid and gullible; she had met him — he had been neither.

The fact still remained: if Myra was the killer, she would have needed help. So the question remained as well: who helped her?

Myra as the killer was fanciful enough; the identity of her accomplice, the only person Regan could come up with in the middle of the night for the role, was even more improbable. She vowed to tell no one her thoughts until she had done some research.

The County Records Department was the perfect place to start.

🏠🏠🏠🏠🏠🏠🏠🏠🏠🏠🏠

Regan was pelted with confetti and dried rose petals as she

waited amid the long line of couples applying for marriage licenses. It was a happy group. There were at least twenty hand-holding duos in various stages of paperwork filling-in, often accompanied by friends documenting the event with their smart phone cameras when the couples, mostly female, were handed their marriage licenses.

The Supreme Court had returned California's Proposition 8 ban on same-sex marriages to the Appellate Court, effectively ending the ban days before, and once the go-ahead was given, pairs, many of whom had been waiting for years for the day they could wed, were preparing to tie the knot.

"Are you with the police, Sheriff's Department, social welfare, attorney's office, or are you a licensed PI?" the harried clerk asked when Regan explained she wanted to see the marriage license of Myra Commons and the adoption papers of her son, Steven Commons Butler. She was trying to formulate an answer that didn't involve lying when the clerk, assuming she must belong to one of those qualifiers, moved on. "You've used our computers before, haven't you?"

Regan reasoned, since she had just used the computer upstairs in Environmental Health to find permits and reports for her clients, it wasn't a complete lie if she answered yes.

"Of course," Regan announced with a little too much conviction. Then she added softly, "Although not for this particular type of search."

"Don't worry. It's straight-forward. You'll figure it out. Computer's over there." The clerk raised her arm and pointed; her underarm, exposed by her sleeveless blouse, jiggled visibly as she bounced her finger up and down to clarify which computer she meant. "Next!"

It took a few minutes, but the Records Department computer allowed searches which, like the searches for property and tax records, followed some predictable logic once she got the hang of it. Besides, after a stint with the obtuse Environmental Health system, Regan could handle anything a county computer could throw at her.

She found a license for Myra Michelle Commons and Francis George Butler dated July 13th — she did the year subtraction in her head quickly — from slightly more than nineteen years ago. It had to be the right marriage license.

Regan had a faster learning curve looking up birth certificates. Steven Commons Butler's certificate was easy to find. She noted the father was listed as Francis George Butler, not Roger Commons. *How curious.*

She started to log out, but changed her mind. As long as she had easy access to vital statistics records, she got into death certificates and entered Roger Commons and the year of Myra's remarriage. There it was, cause of death listed as homicide, a grisly reminder how Stevie's father passed away, and the date of his death.

Myra Butler had applied for a marriage license to her second husband thirty-two days after her first husband was murdered. Regan knew death certificates took thirty days to be issued after a death was reported; Myra and Francis hadn't wasted any time.

Myra and Francis either had the world's fastest meeting and courtship or they were involved before Roger Commons died. Perhaps Myra had decided what was good for the goose was good for the gander, as the saying went, and found her own way of coping with her husband's philandering by lining up husband number two before husband number one was cold.

What she uncovered wasn't proof that Myra was a murderer, but it hinted that if she was, whether Myra called Francis to help her clean up or whether he was involved in murder from the outset, Regan knew who Myra's partner in crime was.

She remained curious about Stevie's birth certificate. Roger Commons must have seen it. Did he and Myra have some sort of agreement or an open marriage? Wouldn't it have been ironic, if rather than Myra being the long suffering wife, Roger Commons turned to other women because his wife was carrying on first?

The line was long, but Regan got back in it. She had to ask the clerk one more question or Stevie's paternity was going to keep her up for a second night. She had her question ready when the clerk's "Next!" was for her.

"Me again," Regan smiled. "I used your computer — you're right, it's easy to use — and found the marriage license and birth certificate I needed. I know there was an adoption, yet I see that the adoptive father's name is the only one on the birth certificate. Does that mean he is the biological father even though the mother was married to someone else when her son was born?"

The clerk blinked and looked confused.

"I'm sorry. You're so busy today, you don't remember me. I'm verifying the marriage license of a widow and the adoption of her son by his step-father," Regan reminded the clerk.

"No. I remember you. When the biological parent is

123

deceased and an adoption takes place, the birth certificate gets changed: the adoptive parent's name gets substituted. Anyone with the right to access those records should know that, so you should know that." The clerk narrowed her eyes. "What I don't remember is your answer about who you're with and why you're qualified to look up those records."

"I didn't say. The truth is I'm just a real estate agent being nosey," Regan answered with complete candor. Then she turned and rushed out of the department like she was sure a ham-handed cop was going to grab her shoulder and arrest her.

She escaped to the security of her car, still blushing at having been caught in subterfuge. Stevie's birth certificate got changed — nothing untoward there — unless Stevie's records weren't changed. What intrigued her when she saw Stevie's birth certificate was still a fascinating possibility, not only because the record might not have been changed, but because changed or not, the certificate might reflect the truth. Remarriage thirty-two days after murder suggested the possibility was real.

Her business with Stevie was concluded; Regan had no plausible reason to see him. After spending a day trying to come up with an elegant excuse to do so, Regan hit on asking him for a friendly field tour of his vineyard. She was certain he had a rudimentary one in by now because, on the day of the unveiling, evidence was visible beyond the house of weed clearing, newly tilled soil, and installed vine supports.

She could start with grapes and easily move the conversation to his mother by asking if Myra had recovered from her fright — Regan caught her breath — her faint. Her faint; better not make a Freudian slip like that in front of Stevie.

Regan didn't expect him to know anything about how or when his mother and Francis got together — he would have been too young to notice their goings-on, and his mother wasn't likely to have shared details, especially titillating ones, with her child — but if Regan controlled the conversation, he might say something about family life that Regan would find significant.

She resorted to his favorite means of communicating,

texting a quick *"R U there & can I see your vines"* message from her office. He responded immediately *"in BD at 2"* Stevie was notoriously late. She arranged her day to free up after 3:00.

🏠🏠🏠🏠🏠🏠🏠🏠🏠🏠🏠

As she climbed the steps and patio landings toward Stevie's front door, she looked left down the sightline of cleared trees toward the future grape-growing field. From her elevated position, she could see Stevie, recognizable because of his hair and stature, out in his infant vineyard supervising several men. She returned to the parking level and began walking toward the vineyard.

A little past halfway through the denuded area, a low cairn of quartz crystals, the milky-white rocks so prevalent in Bonny Doon soil and along its creeks, caught her eye. When she looked up again, Stevie was looking her way, waving her forward with wind-milling sweeps of his arms. She walked faster; he moved in her direction. Within a few more steps, she could see the smile on his face.

"Cool, huh?" he shouted as they converged. "The rocks are from the vineyard. I have my crew stack them as they find them. I'm hoping to go five, six feet high with the quartz. If we find enough, I'll keep only the whitest ones and then have a plaque that points out they're at the resting place of my skeleton. Maybe I'll put a blue light on them so after dark they seem ghostly."

"Oh my," Regan sighed. "You do have a dramatic flair,

although I notice your six-shooter is missing today, and your crew looks like ordinary fieldworkers. No men-in-black?"

Stevie let out a delighted little snigger. "They're nearby, but discrete. It's dumb to have them standing around, so I put them to work around the field perimeter helping my crew string deer fencing. They're not wearing black today, though.

"I don't think I need body guards, anyway. If I was worried, I'd be armed."

"You mean your six-shooter wasn't just for show? You know how to use it?"

"Well, yeah it was, but I know how to use it. I'm almost as good a shot as my dad. And it's a 357 Magnum that holds seven rounds, not some old-westy six-shooter. It's a cop gun; you can ask your friend."

"How did you get competent using a cop gun?"

"My dad taught me. He's a retired cop."

Regan had to work at keeping her surprise from showing. She smiled evenly as she contemplated Francis Butler as a cop who helped his adulterous mistress kill her husband. After knowing Dave and what *to protect and to serve* meant to him, the idea of a murderer working within police ranks, though not unheard of, didn't feel good.

"My mom's worried about the sniper. She thought everything was okay at the unveiling because she knew there were guards scattered throughout my guests and out of sight around the perimeter on the lookout for John Miller, but when the class showed their reconstructions — well, you saw who they looked like, didn't you? Don't you think the guy in the ground is John Miller? Now she wants me to stay indoors because she says who knows who took a shot at me ..."

Regan's theory about Myra getting Francis to help her cover her murderous tracks began collapsing.

"... but I agree with my dad: a sniper would have to be close, because even if a sharpshooter was technically able to take me down at 800 yards, he'd never get off a shot like that with all the woods on my property.

"Dad says I only need guys out a few yards past the start of my trees. That's where my bodyguards are now, helping nail this really great vinyl coated deer fencing I got at the UCSC Arboretum — it's what they use to keep the deer off their grounds — onto the trees with my crew.

"So I'm safe, and not stuck inside or covered in Kevlar like my mom wants. And as soon as the fence gets up, my vines will be safe, too. It's all good. Come and see."

In Regan's mind, Myra was losing ground rapidly as her prime suspect. Was it possible Myra met Francis after her husband's death when he was assigned to the case? If their meeting happened that way, the couple would still have set some kind of record for getting involved, but if Myra was already unhappy in her marriage and Francis was available and attracted to her, perhaps thirty-two days was possible.

"Why didn't you tell me your dad knows my friend Dave," Regan asked as they walked to the vineyard.

"He doesn't."

"But you said he was a cop. Dave seems to know every law enforcement person in the county."

"My dad worked in San Jose. Besides, he was on the swat team. That's elite stuff. He wouldn't be hanging with an ordinary cop like your friend even if they worked in the same town."

Stevie's pride was overcome by enthusiasm when they reached the vineyard. He raced into a spirited narrative. "I'm doing Sangiovese to start. It'll be years before I can harvest enough to be self-sufficient, but I hooked up with this grower who promised to sell me grapes for the next five years so I can make wine right away. I hope we know for sure that it's John Miller's body by the time I bottle in the fall. I can always call the wine Murderer's Brew or something vague like that, but it would be better if I had a name for the label."

On the drive home from Stevie's, Regan scratched Myra Butler off her suspects list. Myra wasn't afraid of John Miller, not because she knew he was dead, but because precautions had been taken to keep her son safe from him. She didn't faint because her painstaking framing of Miller was about to unravel; she fainted because she realized her son was still at risk and that protecting him from an unknown assailant would be harder than keeping him out of John Miller's rifle sight.

Myra's name came off Regan's suspect list, but Francis Butler's name not only remained on it, but assumed the top spot. The motives for murder that she thought fit Myra worked with Francis, as well — only he might have been able to pull off all the murders by himself without Myra knowing anything about it.

He and Myra could have been a couple like she imagined. Their involvement might even have gone back far enough for

Stevie's birth certificate to reflect the truth about his heritage: Francis Butler *could* be Stevie's biological father.

A ground squirrel hesitated by the side of the road. At the last minute he made a run for it and Regan had to hit her brakes hard. The little animal panicked and ran back in the direction he had come from.

Like the squirrel, Regan backtracked, as well. *Umm, no,* she told herself. In the bright light of day, Francis as Stevie's father seemed unlikely. If he was, Myra would have had no reason to stay with her husband; it made more sense that Myra's marriage produced Stevie.

Regan imagined Myra and Francis arguing about their future. She could see him pressing and encouraging her to file for divorce — and she could see Myra putting it off for the sake of family. Regan knew firsthand how hard it was to end a marriage, especially when there were children involved; she'd struggled with that decision herself as a young mother in an unhappy union.

Francis might have hit his breaking point and decided the only way he'd get to marry the woman he loved was if he made her a widow. He could have followed Roger Commons as he went about his real estate business, waiting for him to wind up at a secluded country property, figuring there he'd have all the privacy and opportunity he'd need for his kill.

Mrs. Miller might have picked a bad time to come home from an outing and happened on the murder. Regan could only too clearly imagine the poor woman, terrified and screaming, running for her bedroom and being caught there.

After that, all her ideas about John Miller finding his wife, getting her blood on him, and being killed and buried in the woods so it would look like he fled, still worked.

Even Francis firing the shot at Stevie worked. There were so many people at the winery opening that Francis, the former swat team marksman, could have easily slipped away unnoticed, set up in the woods, and taken his shot. He could have returned his rifle to his car in the commotion that followed the attack. No one was checking car trunks as vehicles arrived or left; it would have been easy for him to smuggle in his weapon and just as easy for him to take it away.

If Francis did the shooting, Stevie would never have been in danger. John Miller, or rather perpetuating the myth about him, would have been Francis's real target. Francis could have intended to have his shot fly safely over Stevie's head or more likely explosively zing into a step or a nearby brick. Either way, panic would ensue and it would have been assumed, especially after Stevie's provocative declaration, that John Miller tried to kill him but missed.

Neither Tom nor the dignitary near Stevie was seriously injured. She wondered if Francis was so good he planned their wounds or if both of them had simply inched into the firing line as he squeezed the trigger.

Regan hated the idea of a cop turned killer, coming as she did from a family filled with generations of proud-to-serve-policemen, but everything worked.

She turned right instead of left when she reached Bonny Doon Road. Regan wasn't going home after all; she needed the cell phone coverage Highway 1 offered so she could catch Dave before he left work. Her theories worked so well, she was ready to tell him what she had uncovered and pieced together.

The bars on her phone went from a flickering one to a strong five as she made the turn toward Santa Cruz at Bonny Doon Beach. Dave didn't pick up until after the fourth ring. When he did, he sounded winded.

"Dave Everett," he puffed.

"It's Regan. We need to talk. I can be to your office in fifteen minutes; will you wait for me? I'm ready to tell you who killed all those people at the Murder House."

She detected a little chuckle before he spoke. "How can I turn down an offer like that? I'll be here for a while anyway. I'm moving, hauling furniture to my new office. I finally get a space fitting for my position on the force. You can help me hang pictures and certificates of merit. Realtors are good at that, aren't they? Don't you guys give one another awards all the time and plaster them all over your office walls so you can look impressive for your clients?"

A visitor badge was waiting for her when she got to the police station on Center Street. The officer at the desk aimed her upstairs and told her the most direct route to Dave's new office was to turn left at the elevator and go all the way down the hall to the back of the building.

"Very nice," Regan offered when she walked through the open door to greet Dave, who sat smiling behind his desk. "It's bigger than a postage stamp. Oh, and it has a window, too."

"A window with a second story view," he corrected, motioning for her to have a look.

"Is that an auto repair shop or a used car lot across the

street? It's kind of hard to tell from here," she teased as she took in his vista. "No, really, it's nice. Good light; airy is a feature that impresses realtors."

"So, we're gonna have a little quid pro quo here: I impress you with my new headquarters and you impress me by solving Bonny Doon's unsolved murders. Give me a name."

"Don't you want to know how I figured it out?"

"Doesn't matter what I want. You're gonna tell me anyway."

Regan tried hard to say Francis Butler and no more, but she couldn't do it. "At first I thought the killer was Stevie's mother, Myra Butler, and that her husband, her second husband — the man who married the widow Commons a mere thirty-plus days after her first husband's murder — helped her dispose of John Miller's body. I thought she killed Miller and buried him — that she and Francis Butler killed him and buried him in the woods by the Murder House — so it would seem John Miller killed his wife and Myra's first husband."

When Regan paused to take a breath, Dave signaled for her to stop by waving his hands in front of his chest.

"It's good I know the players and the history in your little litany or I'd be lost. You think the killer is Myra Butler?"

"… Thought … It struck me as suspicious that she remarried so quickly. If she was the killer, she'd have needed help getting John Miller's body to his grave, so I figured she and Francis Butler must have been having an affair, and that getting rid of her first husband so she could marry Francis was her motive for murder. But I don't think she was involved in the killings anymore."

"You lay awake nights coming up with this stuff, do you?"

"Sometimes," she confessed.

Dave propped his hand up with an elbow on his desk, covered his mouth with his hand, and rubbed. Regan couldn't tell if he was trying to cover a smile or if his pose indicated he was spellbound. She suspected it was the former.

"You're laughing at me, aren't you?"

"No." His voice was too high pitched to be believable, but he frowned and feigned a sympathetic look. "No, I'm not." He pinched his lip with his teeth for added gravity and shook his head slowly for emphasis.

"Now, Regan, just to be clear here," he said slowly, "you no longer think the Butler did it?"

Regan groaned. "Actually, I do think the Butler did it, Francis Butler, though, not Myra Butler. I'm sorry he's the killer, too, because he's one of your own. That's why it all works so well. Stevie says his step-father retired after a career on the San Jose PD swat team. That means he's a great shot. I think he fired at Stevie at the winery opening, knowing it would look like John Miller came out of hiding and tried to kill Stevie because he was angry at him."

"Are you saying Frank Butler — he goes by Frank, not Francis — took a shot at his adopted son?"

"Not at him. He shot near him, to make it seem like he was trying to shoot him, which he wasn't."

Regan paused in her explanation. Dave had said two things she didn't expect. He corrected her about Francis Butler's name. That meant Dave had more of a connection with Stevie's step-father than she realized. More importantly, he knew Stevie had been adopted by Francis Butler. That meant he already knew a lot more about her prime suspect than she thought.

"See now, I can see the wheels turning in your head. No. Not turning. Spinning."

Dave oozed satisfaction. Regan recognized his expression; she'd seen him look like that on other occasions right before he pulled the proverbial rug out from under her feet.

"You're not bad at this crime solving thing, you know. Well, really you are, but it's not your fault. You have to jump to conclusions without knowing all the facts. Tell you what I'm willing to do. If you want to give up your real estate career and come to work for us as an unpaid volunteer, I can get you a small office on the first floor that's recently become available."

He was her friend. Her reaction didn't rise to the level of a sneer, but it came close. "What don't I know?"

"About this case or in gener ..." he fired back and then stopped himself.

Dave looked sheepish, "You know I didn't mean that. I try not to go overboard, but sometimes you dangle such great openings in front of me, I can't always resist.

"You remember how I've told you we always look at the grieving spouse first? We took a good look at the widow Commons all those years ago and ruled her out way back when."

"What about Francis — Frank — Butler? Did you look at him, too?"

"We were looking at him for a while, before John Miller stole the show. You were right about him and Mrs. Butler — Myra Commons at the time of the first murders. Seems they went to high school together and always liked one another but never got to be a couple, at least not until their ten-year reunion. Mrs. B, then Mrs. C, was unhappy in her marriage because her hubby had an eye for the ladies — more than just an eye.

"At the reunion, she shared her sad story with Frank — really wound up the knight in shining armor in him because she was pregnant by the cheating husband and because he already had a soft spot for her — and after the reunion, they started talking on the phone so he could console her. You get the picture."

"I knew they were involved before the murders," Regan said triumphantly. "Does that mean the police suspected him of killing Roger Commons so he could have Myra all along?"

"Why would he have to kill Commons?"

"Because Myra wouldn't leave her husband, probably for her baby's sake," Regan offered.

"Mrs. B/C was only too happy to leave hubby number one, once she identified hubby number two. Her divorce from Commons would have been final if he lived another couple of weeks."

"Myra was divorcing Roger when he was killed?" Regan asked, "But then my theory… was there a financial incentive? Would Myra do better as a widow than she would have as a divorcee?"

"Not really. True, as a widow Mrs. B/C would get outright ownership of family assets, but there'd be no child support from a dead husband and the Commons were a young family; they didn't have much except a leased car and a house with a big mortgage.

"Now that I'm beginning to feel a little guilty for shooting you down again, I better tell you the rest of the story. There's something big you don't know. Today's news is a game-changer, or a game-unchanger. Whatever."

Regan leaned across Dave's desk eagerly.

"Remember how when you thought John Miller was the guy buried in the woods, I bet you 'ole Jake Miller would be only too happy to give us some DNA for a match if he thought he could clear his brother's name?"

"Yes. Did he?"

"He sure did. Our lead guy on the case gave him a call and asked him to come on down. Seems Jake was hopping on a flight out of the area for a three-week business trip so he couldn't make it to Santa Cruz, but he did the next best thing. Before he got on his flight, he ran by a police station in San Francisco near where he lives and got swabbed."

Dave leaned across his desk toward Regan to match her pose.

"We got the results this morning. No familial match," Dave said softly before he leaned back in his chair once more.

"So as unlikely as it seems, the guy buried in the woods is still just some guy in the woods: an unknown — and coincidental — murder victim.

"Looks like you were right the first time. John Miller is still out there. He's the one who attacked you and took that shot at your little weirdo. The Butler kid's just lucky Miller isn't as good a shot as Frank Butler is."

"And on the next hole, I shot another hole-in-one, and then on the fifteenth and sixteenth, I did it again." Tom watched as Regan listlessly poked at the baked potato on her plate, ignoring the nonsensical details he was using to test whether she was paying attention. "Sweetheart, where are you tonight?"

She looked up at him with big eyes. "What?

"Where are you? You're sure not here with me having dinner."

"I know; I'm sorry."

"You want to tell me about it?"

"I already told you everything there is to tell. Jake Miller's DNA isn't a match for the Murder House skeleton. If that's true, it means John's still alive and well, unpunished for the murders he's committed, and free to continue taking pot-shots at Stevie."

"You said the police were keeping an eye on him and that he and his family have been advised. Stevie has the resources to take care of himself until the police get Miller. And they will."

"If the police could find him, wouldn't they have by now? It's been almost twenty years since this all started and they haven't caught him yet. There's been no justice for Inez and Josh Miller or for Josh's mother and Roger Commons."

"He's kept a low profile for most of those years; now he's come out of hiding and gotten everyone's attention. They'll get him now."

Regan forced a smile for her husband. "You're probably right."

"Probably? Aren't you the woman who thinks I'm logical, brilliant, and always right?"

"Logical and brilliant, yes, but always right? Umm," her smile changed from strained to sassy, "that's pushing it. Thanks for trying, though."

"Trying?"

"To brighten my outlook."

"Trying? Not succeeding?" he cajoled.

The corners of her mouth turned up, but she shook her head. "There's just something not right about this whole thing. Until I figure out what it is ..." she sighed.

"I keep going back to the facial reconstructions. You saw them. Tell me you didn't see Jake Miller's face."

"DNA doesn't lie, sweetheart. The skeleton's not John Miller. Remember what Stevie said before the unveilings? He said that facial reconstruction, while grounded in science and statistical measurement, is still a highly subjective art form, kind of an educated artistic guess, if you will.

"Didn't he bring the class members to the gravesite before they began working on their reconstructions? He may have done so inadvertently, but I bet if you look into it, you'd find

139

he influenced the outcome of their work in some way. If you can't let it go — which is what I think you should do — why don't you ask him what he said to the students."

"This time you are right," she said mischievously. "That's what I'll do." Regan attacked her potato with renewed vigor.

"The let it go part or the talk to Stevie part?"

"Talking to Stevie. He loves melodrama and he badly wants to use his ghost in the woods as part of the label for his first wine offering. I can imagine him setting up tripods with a poster-sized blowup of Josh, Inez, his father, and Mrs. Miller, maybe even John Miller, too — yes, of course John's photo would be there. In Stevie's mind he'd want to have all the principle players in the murders represented.

"I can just hear him telling the class a good ghost story about what happened in the house and how the neighbors reported seeing the specter of a woman in the upstairs window and a ball of light in the woods near the gravesite. He'd tell them John Miller killed all those people — it's what he believes happened — he'd be memorable; the students would have his image in the back of their minds."

Regan put her hand on Tom's neck, pulled him to her, and gave him a kiss. "You're right. He could have planted a suggestion — planted the image the students came up with — without ever suggesting how their busts should look. I'll ask him how he primed the class and, hopefully, put my uneasiness to rest.

"It's wonderful being married to such a brilliant and usually right man," she giggled.

"And, add a man who is looking forward to many more years of marriage to the woman he loves: an amateur sleuth who has solved her mystery and can get back to her real life."

🏠🏠🏠🏠🏠🏠🏠🏠🏠🏠🏠

The next morning, Regan called Stevie. It was an act of loop closing, no more. She planned to ask him a few questions, confirm that he subliminally or directly conveyed John Miller's likeness to his reconstruction class, and firmly set her mind to rest like Tom suggested.

Stevie's phone rang and went to answering mode. She texted him in case he was playing phone contact games. *Your cell isn't working. Call me.*

When he didn't respond quickly, she assumed that, even though it was the weekend, he was probably out in his field flapping his arms madly at men planting grape vines and wouldn't get back to her until the sun set.

She tried him on Sunday and again got his outgoing message. By Monday morning, when he still hadn't returned her call, she deemed him the most self-centered twenty-one-year-old homeowner she knew and decided that, if she wanted her questions answered, she'd have to take Bonny Doon Road — an annoying addition of twenty minutes on her commute — and swing by his house on the way to her office.

As Regan turned up Stevie's driveway, she almost collided with a gold colored Buick, vintage late 80's she guessed, coming down the driveway too fast to be stopped by any but the best of brakes. She swerved hard right off the paved portion of the drive and stopped, hoping her move was enough of an adjustment to keep the cars apart. The oncoming Buick, which already sported a rusted dent in the left front fender as evidence of past driving indiscretions, barreled down the center of the driveway without a corresponding concession.

She glared at the driver, willing him to slow so that she could fully communicate her anger at being forced into the scratchy roadside brush. Her vexation and telegraphed anger didn't lighten his gas pedal foot. The Buick passed her so close that Regan expected, if nothing else, that their side-view mirrors would collide. Only an offsetting difference in the mirrors' height saved them.

A Jake Miller look-a-like glared back at her with wide-eyed defiance. Her heart felt like it was about to freeze in her chest.

"Stevie," she cried his name out loud and gunned her Prius toward his house.

Before she reached the parking area in front of his steps, she had made a cruel triage-like decision. It was unlikely the Buick driver was Jake Miller, but if he was, Stevie was fine. If the driver was John Miller — unfortunately the likely reality — in spite of Stevie's precautions, given John's track record and his hasty exit, she was too late. Stevie was already dead.

She circled her car around in the parking area and started down the driveway, moving as quickly as the Buick had moments before, while she entered 9-1-1 on her hands-free device and hoped for a cell phone miracle. Cell phones might not support chat in Bonny Doon, but she had once heard that the emergency number was supposed to connect at all times. It wasn't true.

Her car hit the driveway intersection with the road, and like it had been when she was fleeing the night she was attacked, her car was tossed out of her control. This time she was prepared for the experience. Although she let out a cry, she regained control immediately and turned right as she had seen the Buick do in her rear view mirror.

When she reached Bonny Doon Road, she tried to think like a fleeing killer: If he turned left into the greater part of Bonny Doon, he would have a myriad of hiding places, but Bonny Doon could be sealed off. If he turned right, he would reach Highway 1 in minutes, and while that main traffic artery could be blockaded as well, if the killer had twenty minutes to make it past Santa Cruz in one direction or Gazos Creek Road between the communities of Davenport and Pescadero in the other, he would have many escape options. She thought John Miller would choose the open road; she turned right and aimed down Bonny Doon Road toward the coast.

She drove too fast, but she knew the road almost as well as Empire Grade, her normal route to Santa Cruz. Unless her quarry was driving as recklessly as she was, she must be closing the gap between them. Regan clutched her steering wheel with tense hands and looked hard at the road in front of her, hoping to see a large gold-colored vehicle after each turn in the road.

She couldn't see the ocean or Highway 1, even from her altitude, but she knew it was there. The surrounding trees were lower and more open, too; she checked her hands-free device again. It registered a single solid bar with a second bar flickering on and off. She hit the redial button and prayed.

"9-1-1," a woman's voice came over her speaker, "What is your location and emergency?" she asked with calm efficiency. Regan gave Stevie's address. "And your emergency?" the calm voice repeated.

"I think there's been a murder. I'm trying to follow the killer. He's in an old gold-colored Buick. I'll try to stay on his trail long enough to see where he's going. If I can get close enough, I'll report his license plate number."

"Ma'am, are you all right?"

"I'm fine. Please send help to where I told you."

"Help is on the way, ma'am. It is not a good idea for you to pursue ..." the calm voice sounded less so, "a criminal. It would be best for you to return to the address you gave and wait there."

"Not a chance!" Regan surprised herself with her sudden resolve. "This guy has killed before and disappeared. I don't want him to get away this time. I'll call back when I have something useful to tell you."

"That isn't a good idea."

Regan pressed the END button on her phone. She agreed with the 9-1-1 operator, but she had made up her mind. The last thing she wanted to listen to was a voice of reason trying to dissuade her.

She spotted the Buick ahead where the road overlooked a wide curve just after she passed the sign warning of an upcoming 10% grade and a twisting road for the next four miles.

Regan didn't see the small gray van between them until she rounded the next curve and almost overtook it. The rear window of the auto was resplendent with stickers announcing its occupants might include a man, a woman, two boys, a baby girl, two dogs, a cat, and a turtle.

It appeared the woman was driving today. She was cautious and hit her breaks frequently to maintain what she must have deemed a sensible speed of no more thirty miles-per-hour. Passing was an impossibility given the road. Regan pounded on her horn. The woman slowed to twenty-five.

A frustrated Regan didn't catch a glimpse of the Buick again until she and the turtle van reached the stop sign at the intersection with Highway 1 across the road from Bonny Doon Beach. She hesitated at the stop sign pondering which way she should turn — which direction the killer would have taken — when she saw the car parked almost opposite from her. She crossed Highway 1 and pulled her car in behind the Buick.

Bonny Doon Beach was a secluded but still popular summer destination. Even on a Monday morning, most of the parking spaces were full. All of the other spaces close to the beach access were taken. An open spot so near the trail head conveniently waiting to be filled by the Buick was unlikely. John Miller had probably double parked like she had, backed out a car he had left at the beach — one that he had driven away recently — and moved the Buick into the vacated space.

He was gone, and she had no idea which direction he had taken or what he was driving. She had no useful information to help the authorities be on the lookout for him. John Miller had disappeared once more.

Regan got back in her car and started back up Bonny Doon Road, knowing she had to return to the Murder House and hoping that by the time she got there, police and EMTs would have beaten her back to the house, and no one would let her see Stevie's body.

The scene she pulled up to at his house wasn't what she expected. There was no crime scene tape up or ambulance parked outside, and certainly no coroner's van. There was a police car — only one — and an unharmed Stevie, with his unmistakable almost white hair, standing on one of the patio risers interspersed among his front steps, cradling a phone between his shoulder and ear.

He finished his conversation and waved to her cheerily as she bounded up the steps toward him. "Stevie, you're not dead," she hollered.

She held up her arms ready to hug him, but he backed away, pink spots forming in his cheeks. "Uh, no," he stated the obvious derisively.

"I thought I saw ... but you're okay. What a relief."

"Are you the one who called 9-1-1? I got a call from an operator asking if I needed police and an ambulance. She said a woman called in an emergency. I told her to send the police because there was a robbery, but no one was hurt."

A bewildered Regan frowned. "A robbery, not ..."

Stevie launched into his narrative over her words. "Juan, that's the farm worker's name, said this guy came by the housing where he lives and asked if anybody there had a car and wanted to earn a quick hundred. He said all they had to do was deliver a message. Juan has a car and could use the money, so he stepped up.

"The man asked Juan to give him a five-minute head start

and then pick him up at the bottom of Bonny Doon Road. When Juan got there, the guy wanted to drive. Juan didn't like that idea, but the man gave him another hundred to make him happy, so Juan went along."

"That explains the car," Regan interjected.

Stevie didn't seem to notice. "So, they came up here and Juan knocked on my door. When I opened it and saw him, I thought he heard about my vine planting and was looking for work. Before I could ask him, the guy in his car takes off and Juan starts running after him, yelling for him to stop.

"I grabbed my gun and started running and yelling stop, too. At first, I think Juan thought I was after him because he looked scared to death, like he thought I was gonna shoot him. But then he realized I was trying to get his car back so he calmed down and came back in the house with me to call the cops. Right about then, I thought I saw you spin around in my parking lot in your green Prius and head back down my driveway.

"We were about to make the call when I got the 9-1-1 operator asking me questions. A few minutes later, a cop car pulls up. Man, those 9-1-1 operators are fast. I always heard it took twenty minutes for the police to think about sending anyone to Bonny Doon, but he came right away.

"The cop is inside with Juan taking down the description of his missing car and the guy who stole it. His Buick was old, but he can't replace it with only two hundred dollars and he needs it to get to work. He's bummed."

"I followed an old Buick from your place to Bonny Doon Beach. It's parked there now."

"You found Juan's car?" Stevie's baby-toothed smile burst

across his face. "I gotta tell him."

Stevie capered toward his front door with Regan a step behind him.

"Hey man, she found your car. El hombre no robó su coche. Es en la playa."

"You find my car?"

Regan nodded.

The man smiled, revealing a gap where one of his front teeth should be. "Gracias. Thank you."

Stevie questioned the officer, "You aren't going to keep it for evidence are you?"

"I don't think that will be necessary, sir. I have what I need to file my report. It's not even clear the car was stolen, considering Mr. Rubio was paid for its use. Anyway, the car has been found, so that should be that."

Juan nodded vigorously, "Sí, sí. Thank you, señor policia." He stood up and shook the officer's hand. Next he took Stevie's hand in both of his and shook it with great vigor. Then he stretched out his hand toward Regan, "Muchas gracias, señora. I go to my car now."

"Wait!" Regan disrupted the round robin of hand shaking. "What about John Miller? I saw him driving Mr. Rubio's car. Miller must have left his car at the beach so he could trade back to it and make a clean getaway after the note was delivered. Officer, he's killed four people — right here, in this house."

"Dios mío!" Juan made the sign of the cross, "He is in my car!"

"The note," Stevie said, reaching into his back pocket. "I forgot about that."

He read it quickly and then offered a summary of what it said. "The note *is* from John Miller. He says he's giving me one last chance to stop disrespecting him. He says if I use his name to sell my wine, I'm going to die like all those others."

"What a coward," Stevie sounded disappointed. "I was ready for him to try and kill me. Instead he only gave me a warning, and not even in person."

The police officer cleared his throat, "Well then, I'm afraid we may need to impound Mr. Rubio's car and your note. John Miller has a felony murder arrest warrant out on him; we'll need the car and note as evidence."

Mr. Rubio groaned.

"Señor, I'll drive you home, voy a su casa. Y mañana trabajar por mi," Stevie offered in broken Spanish. "You can work for me as long as you don't have a car, usted es sin coche."

🏠🏠🏠🏠🏠🏠🏠🏠🏠🏠🏠

Regan dangled a bulging bakery bag in front of Tom and swung it back and forth in small arcs like a hypnotist putting a patient into a trance.

"Really big sandwiches from Kelly's," she said. "I need to walk fast and talk faster and I'm starving. Seeing John Miller has made me hungrier than usual. I thought we could head toward Natural Bridges State Beach. I know it's not the right time of year for them, but we can cut through the eucalyptus grove and take a shortcut on the Monarch Boardwalk, see if there are any straggler butterflies left hanging in the trees, and have a picnic. Please say you can go missing from the office for a couple of hours."

"I can get away, no problem."

"In addition to being as hungry as I've ever been in my life, I have an unbearable amount of nervous energy to burn. Let's go; let's walk."

"Before we look for butterflies," Tom drew a figure eight in the air with his index finger, "you want to back up to the part where you thought you saw John Miller and tell me about that?"

"Saw him, not thought I saw him. I've had an exciting morning."

By the time they turned right onto the broadest stretch of Delaware Avenue, Regan was telling Tom about discovering Mr. Rubio's abandoned car.

"What did you intend to do if you caught up with him?"

"I hadn't planned that far ahead," she shrugged. "I was too busy trying to follow him to think beyond stalking my quarry, and as absurd as it seems now, a part of me was still hoping I was following Jake Miller — the man I saw looked like Jake, after all, and not his brother — because of Stevie. I did plan on calling the emergency operator back once I was sure I was on his trail, though. And I wasn't going to do anything dangerous."

"The man's killed four people — you thought he'd just murdered Stevie — isn't trying to get close to him dangerous? Suppose he recognized you or realized you were following him?"

"Jake Miller would recognize me; his brother wouldn't."

"Are you sure about that? If everything fits together like it seems to, Miller would have seen you in your car twice: the night he took out your windows and again today at the Murder House. I don't like you taking risks."

"John Miller kills by getting up close to his victims; I was ready to run away," Regan laughed and grabbed Tom's hand. She took several quick, bouncing steps down the street, dragging him with her.

"All this car chasing seems to have put you in a good mood. You're not uneasy anymore? No more lingering doubts because of the facial reconstructions?"

"You're right, I am in a good mood. I guess that means my doubts are gone. They must be, because like Dave says, there's no familial match between the skeleton's DNA and Jake Miller's. It's never wrong — DNA, I mean — is it?"

"I don't think so."

"And I saw John Miller alive and in the flesh, and he signed the note Mr. Rubio gave to Stevie, too."

"Not only that," Tom said, "the police will probably match fingerprints from the car steering wheel or from the note; they must have Miller's on file from the first murders. That should seal the deal, no loose ends."

"Except for catching him. Until that happens, I'm still going to worry about Stevie. He wants justice. He'll bait Miller, he'll be the bait himself if that's what he thinks it takes to get him. He has a just cause and the invincibility of youth on his side, a dangerous enough coupling, and he also thinks he's smarter than everyone in the room, certainly cleverer than John Miller."

"Isn't he?"

"Probably. I just hope he isn't too smart for his own good.

"Dave asked me to come into the station and sit with a sketch artist. The police have a photo of Miller that's twenty years old. They think it could be helpful to know what he looks like now."

"When are you going in? I would think the sooner the better, while his face is still clear in your mind."

"I'm not going in immediately. I have a clear memory of the man I saw; he looked like Jake Miller. It was strange to look at the killer and see his brother, but I guess it's not surprising that they've aged similarly, given how closely they resembled one another as younger men.

"I asked Dave for some time before I see the sketch artist. What I would like to do is see Jake Miller again, look at him closely, and see if I can spot differences between the man I saw today and him. I'll look for dissimilarities. Once I have them in mind, meeting with a sketch artist will be more productive.

"The only problem is, after the way things ended when Stevie bought the Murder House, I doubt he'll agree to sit still while I stare at him. He may not want to help me come up with a better description of his brother, either, blood being thicker than water and all that.

"I've contacted his office; Jake's due back at work on Wednesday after being away on business. What do you think I should do? Should I call him and ask if he'll see me or drop by his office in the City unannounced?"

"Aren't we overdue for a great dinner in San Francisco? Wednesday is our day off; if you want a little face-time with Miller, I vote we spend it taking a ride to The City and surprise him," Tom winked.

They timed their arrival at Jake Miller's office for 4:45 on Wednesday. Based on what their business lives were like on the first day back in the office after a time away, they knew he would be busy most of the day. But by 4:45, he should be winding down, tired perhaps, but alone in his office.

"You're my assistant," Tom announced as they took the elevator to the fifth floor at number 2 Pine. "And if there are any problems, they're your fault. Be prepared: I'm a mean boss."

"Will you want me to shed a tear if you treat me badly or would that be too much? Maybe I shouldn't break down and cry, just get moist eyes?"

"You can do that on cue?"

Regan smiled up at him impishly, "I think so."

Tom opened the door with J. Miller Investments stenciled on it. He let himself in first, leaving Regan trailing behind him.

"Thomas Kiley for Mr. Miller. I'm sorry I'm late. I've come all the way from Santa Cruz. Traffic was terrible."

The receptionist clicked her mouse a couple of times. "I'm

153

sorry sir. I don't see your name on the appointment ..."

"K-i-l-e-y," Tom spelled.

"No, Mr. Kiley. This is Mr. Miller's first day back at work after an extended business trip. He asked me to keep his appointments to a minimum. You're not here."

"Clearly I am here." He turned to Regan and boomed, "You told me you made the appointment."

"I ... I did, Mr. Kiley." She looked distraught as she pleaded with the receptionist. "Can't we see him? Please?"

"Of course we can. Through here?" Tom demanded.

"Yes, but ..." the receptionist started ineffectually.

"Thank you," Tom's gratitude was sarcastic.

"Now I know how Amanda felt when Jake Miller's attorney forced his way past her," Regan whispered as they headed for the inner office door, leaving the receptionist on the intercom, struggling to hastily prepare her boss for unexpected visitors.

Regan was steeled for confronting Jake Miller; she got a gentle smile instead of anger.

"Mrs. McHenry, Mr. Kiley. We meet again. Let me start by apologizing for my past abruptness. It's only that I was so concerned about your client, Mr. Butler. I know you were doing your best for both of us," he sighed. "Ah well, the purchase is concluded, and if something happens to him it's ... it's beyond our control now, isn't it?

"The police called to ask if I had heard from my brother. They told me what happened recently. I reiterated that my brother has never contacted me since ... since the beginning."

"I saw him," Regan said, "as he was leaving Stevie's house. He passed me on the driveway."

Jake Miller's face flushed. "This will sound horrible. I had such great hope that the skeleton was my brother's, even after the police told me there was no familial match with my DNA. In some ways it would have been easier to accept his death — his murder — than his life. But you saw him?" Jake Miller's blue eyes bore into hers. "Are you sure it was him?"

Regan nodded.

"Tell me, did you see him clearly? Did he look well? I know what he's done; I know what he's capable of doing, but he's still my brother. I still care about him," his voice quavered and fell to a barely perceptible murmur, "even after Josh."

At the mention of Josh, Regan bit her lip. The moisture in her eyes that she had teasingly told Tom she could produce at will was real. "He looked as well as you do," she said gently.

"He looked remarkably like you, in fact. The police want me to meet with a sketch artist to produce a current image of him. I wanted to see you first, but I thought you wouldn't agree to a meeting if I asked." She felt manipulative and thoughtless, "So we came up with this ruse to get inside your office."

Regan glanced at Tom. He looked as sheepish as she felt. "Please apologize to your receptionist for us, will you?" he asked. "We steamrolled her."

"I wanted to study your face. I thought if I did, I could better tell the sketch artist how to modify a photo of you to make it look like your brother. I'm sorry. I know how hard it must be for you to help with his capture."

"It has to be done," Jake Miller's voice was firm, but filled with sorrow.

"We looked so much alike when we were young that people often asked if we were twins. Of course there were differences between us. I was taller and in all ways bigger than he was; it often happens that the second son grows bigger than his older brother, doesn't it? John had brown eyes and mine are blue. And his hair was lighter than mine, but not much lighter. I'm gray now; he probably would be, too.

"Our differences would be hard to see unless we were side-by-side. You can look at me as closely as you want, Mrs. McHenry. I doubt it will help you."

They stopped for dinner at Absinthe, a popular restaurant in San Francisco's Hayes Valley district. The noise level was high, but it was still a romantic spot; hearing over the din forced faces close together and reassured patrons that their intimate conversations remained private. The tables-for-two sported crisp white linens long enough to hide discreet under-table touching and were topped with modest candles which didn't get in the way of cross-table hand-holding or staring intently into one another's eyes.

Tom and Regan did a fair amount of what the restaurant encouraged. Regan was especially drawn to her husband's intensely blue eyes, gazing into them deeply and often. She seemed able to divert her own eyes for only moments before the magnetism of his eyes pulled her back into their depths.

They leaned toward one another and spoke in whispers. The well-trained servers, unlike so many in their profession who seemed to interrupt at just the worst time, hung back thoughtfully, giving Tom and Regan privacy.

Regan drew even closer to her husband, puckered her lips

and blew softly. The candles that separated them flickered and died. He moved inexorably toward her, his head tilted back slightly.

Her voice was bewitching and soft. She enunciated each word carefully. "I'm absolutely certain the driver had blue eyes."

"You said he went by you quickly and you were under a great deal of stress. You couldn't see him well enough to tell the color of his eyes."

"I am a blue-eyed aficionado, thanks to you. I notice blue eyes. Even when I'm not conscious of doing it, I compare the shades I see in other blue eyes to yours. You're right about rapidity and lighting: it does make it harder to tell, but even in the low light here now that the candle is out, I know your eyes are blue. It was full daylight at Stevie's and the driver came very close to me.

"I can still see if a person's eyes are blue under challenging conditions, and Jake Miller said his brother's eyes were brown."

"So you think it was Jake Miller at Stevie's, impersonating his brother, even though he was away on business at the time?"

"A mere detail," she smiled coyly.

"A major obstacle," Tom replied seriously. "Besides, why would he do it?"

"That is the million-dollar question, isn't it? The man I saw definitely had blue eyes, though. I'm sure of it, so it had to be Jake Miller."

Regan's mind was hard at work. She neglected her dinner. "Other things beside eye color point to the man I saw being

157

Jake, not John. Monday's Miller gave Stevie a written and signed warning. John Miller kills people, he doesn't write threatening letters to them.

"His murders have been bloody; every time I think of him," she shuddered involuntarily, "I see him covered with his victim's blood. After he ... finishes, he hides. In the past, he's been secretive, stealthy. He's slipped away and waited for his victims to be discovered. But this time he was boldfaced in going to a farm laborer camp, borrowing a car, signing a note, and then parking the car he used in a public place. It was like he was saying, 'Hey, everyone, look at me.'

"He changed ... umm ... what do they call it?" Regan searched for the right phrase. "He changed his MO, that's it, what the police call his modus operandi. That tells me he was a different person."

"Or, it could say that he had a reason for behaving differently this time. It could be that since he didn't plan on killing anyone," Tom grimaced in acknowledgement of Regan's bloody imagery, "he didn't think he'd need to get cleaned up this time. That could account for what you're seeing as changed behavior.

"He may have parked in the lot at Bonny Doon Beach because he knew overnight parking isn't allowed and reasoned that the farm worker's car would be spotted and returned to Mr. Rubio — an innocent bystander, after all — before it caused him too much hardship."

Regan's reaction to Tom's suggestion was swift. "That proves my point. You don't think John Miller, a man who kills brutally, would care about inconveniencing Mr. Rubio, do you? Remember Inez was an innocent bystander; it didn't save her life."

"Inez surprised him, caught him in the act," Tom spoke softly as he reached across the table and gently took Regan's hand. "Miller couldn't let her run off and call the police, not if he needed time to cover his tracks and disappear. But he staged his second murders — put his signature on them as it were — so it was obvious who had committed them. He wanted time, not anonymity. He's not being inconsistent.

"You didn't ask Dave if the fingerprints on the car steering wheel and the note match John Miller's yet, did you? I bet they do. No changed MO, no mystery. And no more being so pensive that you're not even tasting this amazing dinner."

🏠🏠🏠🏠🏠🏠🏠🏠🏠🏠🏠

Regan had an appointment with the sketch artist at 1:30. She had more than an hour to kill between showing the last agent around her listing on Thursday morning broker tour and when she was due at the police station.

Tom had tried, but he hadn't talked her out of believing Jake Miller was the man she saw on Monday. To her way of thinking, there was no point in showing up for her appointment; the police could look at a photo of Jake Miller if they wanted to know what the man driving away from the Murder House looked like. Nevertheless, she decided to do what Tom suggested: she'd ask Dave whose fingerprints the police found on the note and Mr. Rubio's steering wheel.

His door was open as usual, but Regan knocked on the door jamb before going into Dave's office.

159

"What's this?" he asked as he spun his desk chair around to face her, a welcoming grin on his face. "You've never knocked on my door before. You usually fly into my space all frantic with your latest imaginings and start yammering before I can tell you to calm down."

"Your new office warrants a more circumspect entrance," she smiled genially, "and another look at its opulence."

Dave narrowed his eyes. "I'd like to believe that, but I know you too well. This visit isn't purely a social call to admire my office. You're up to something or you want something; which is it?"

"You have John Miller's fingerprints on file, don't you?"

"Of course."

"Did the fingerprints on Mr. Rubio's car or on the note Stevie Butler got match them?"

"No fingerprints to match to. The Rubio guy says the man who pulled the mini theft of his car wore gloves. Our letter writer must have done the same when he worked on his note. The paper was run through a computer printer. Miller mustn't be a fanner — no playing with his paper when he puts it in his printer — and must have put on some nice little latex gloves before he took the paper out and folded it up."

Regan crumpled into a seat across from Dave's desk. "Tom thought I'd be proven wrong because you'd find conclusive fingerprint evidence, but I knew there weren't going to be fingerprints."

"So Miller was careful not to leave fingerprints; no big deal. Lots of criminals are careful not to leave fingerprints." Dave frowned, "Proven wrong about what?"

"Solve this conundrum, will you? If you put your name on

a note, why do you wear gloves when you write it?"

Regan watched Dave roll his eyes around as if the answer to her question hung just below the ceiling in his new office, waiting to be discovered. His expression was one of perturbed frustration.

"Maybe he's got a compulsive disorder, you know, instead of washing his hands thirty-seven times in a row, he wears gloves. Why do you care why he didn't want to leave his fingerprints?"

"Because the man I saw driving Mr. Rubio's car wasn't John Miller, it was his brother, Jake, and Jake was careful not to leave fingerprints because he didn't want anyone to know that."

Her declaration drew a disconcerted reaction from him. "Aw, gee, Regan, why do you think that?"

"Because the driver had blue eyes like Jake does. John's eyes were, are," she struggled with whether to place John's eyes in the past or present, "were brown. Jake even said they were. Look up the photo you have of him in the crime file. You'll see."

Dave clicked away on his computer. Regan could tell when he found what he was looking for because he leaned close to his screen and turned his sighted eye toward it.

He clicked again to enlarge the photo. "The description says his eyes are brown, but from looking at the picture you can't tell what color …" He clicked twice more, "well, so what. Look how hard I had to study his picture to tell his eye color. You expect me to believe you could see what color the guy's eyes were through two car windows?"

She made guesses and took leaps of faith more often than

she cared to admit. The results of her speculations were more often problematic than she cared to admit, too, but not this time. She knew who she had seen behind the wheel of Mr. Rubio's car.

She didn't try to answer him. Instead she asked, "Can you tell the color of a person's eyes by looking at their DNA?"

"Where are you going with this, Regan?"

"Can you?" she asked again.

"Most of the time."

"What color eyes did the skeleton in the woods have?"

Her query stopped Dave cold.

"Do you understand the implications of what you're asking?" He was somber and professional, and not her friend. He had become her interrogator, trying to dispassionately determine if she was a credible witness.

The weight of Dave's question hit her with full force. Last night she and Tom had followed a careful script: he tried to convince her that she was mistaken; she focused unwaveringly on her ability to distinguish eye color. They mindfully avoided considering what her being right might mean because Jake Miller pretending to be his brother raised potentially ugly questions.

"I'm beginning to … yes, I do." She sat up as straight as she would on the witness stand. "I'm convinced John Miller is the body in the woods."

Dave tilted his head. "You do know the comparison between Jake Miller's DNA and the skeleton's DNA ruled that out, don't you?" His question sounded like it held more uncertainty than conviction.

"How reliable are those types of comparisons?" she asked.

"Super reliable."

"Even so, I think there's been a mistake. The comparison needs to be done again."

"You want the department to drop another half-grand to rerun the test?"

"No. I think you should get Jake Miller to get a fresh swab first and then run another test. Could you ask him to supply more DNA and try matching it one more time?"

"And if he says, 'why?' and I say, 'because we think you've been impersonating your dead brother and we need a new DNA sample to prove it' and then he says, 'no thanks,' what am I gonna do?"

"Can't you get a warrant or something and make him do it?"

In the next moment she could see his body language shift. He had made his decision: her testimony shouldn't be trusted.

"Yeah," Dave snickered, "easy enough. I'll just go to someone a lot higher up the food chain than I am and say, 'would you mind going to a judge and asking him to compel a man with no criminal background, a pillar of his community, who has always been cooperative and helpful with our investigation, and who has had to live with the loss of family members — including his nephew who was like a son to him — at his brother's hand to give us another DNA sample?'

"And when this mucky-muck asks me why I want him to do that, I get to say, 'because I've got this friend who thinks this guy's eye color is wrong.' Is that really what you want me to do?"

Regan nodded silently.

Dave waved his hands in the air like he was trying to shake water off of them. "Judges don't grant warrants because we ask for one. A judge has to be persuaded there's a reasonable suspicion of guilt before he'll issue a warrant. Asking some judge for a warrant because you think a driver you saw in a hurried drive-by has baby-blues isn't gonna cut it.

"Besides, even if you did see Jake Miller pretending to be his brother, there could be innocent reasons why he wanted to do it."

She was being dismissed and derailed and it was getting her Irish up. The more Dave tried to raise doubt, the more intransigent she became about what she had seen. "Really?" she asked sarcastically. "Tell me one reason."

"Maybe your Miller guy was trying to keep your little weirdo shaken up. The note whichever Miller he was delivered said Butler's using the Miller tragedies for publicity was upsetting him. Butler's antics probably annoy Jake almost as much as John; I could see him wanting to freak out your little freak to get him to back off.

"Messing with your little weirdo; I can relate to that all right. Reminds me of something I'd secretly like to do to that kid." Dave plastered a satisfied grin on his face.

"Why didn't he admit to that, then, when Tom and I saw him? Why did he conduct such a charade, even asking me if his brother looked well?"

"Jake Miller's not that fond of you either, is he? Maybe he was doing a two-fer."

"The only mature," Regan fought to keep from sounding snappish, "the only reason for doing what Jake did that makes sense is that John Miller has been dead for almost twenty years, that his brother knows it, and that he doesn't want anyone else to know it."

Her conclusion had tumbled out before she thought about what she was saying. It surprised even her. Regan expected, maybe even hoped, to be mocked.

Dave's smile disappeared. "This idea of yours makes your 'the Butlers did it' theory look solid by comparison. You're headed down a pretty disturbing road here, one with a big cliff at the end of it, Regan. If big brother was dead, he couldn't have committed the last two killings."

"No, he couldn't." It was time to say out loud what had been unsettling her mind. Regan took a deep breath and jumped off Dave's cliff, "I think Jake Miller is a murderer — the murderer. I think he's responsible for all the Murder House deaths, including his brother's."

Dave blew up so suddenly that she jumped in her seat. He slapped his hand on his desk, "You think a man without a motive has one. You think the DNA match was botched. You think Jake Miller is a brutal murderer. All that because you think you saw blue eyes in the blur of a passing car instead of brown eyes?

"I got another quick question for you, too. If Jake wanted everyone to believe his brother was alive, why point out the difference in eye color to you and Tom? Seems like that would be asking for trouble, which is what he's getting from you, now, isn't it?

"I'll apologize later for yelling at you and you'll accept my apology because we're still friends, but right now — out — out of my new office. No more putting me in the middle of your crazy ideas. Don't come see me here again until you find another hobby that doesn't involve playing amateur detective."

Regan didn't say a word — she might regret her words as much as she was sure he would regret his once he calmed down — instead she stood up, accepted her banishment, and headed for his door.

She paused in the doorframe and looked back at him, hoping he was already feeling a pang of guilt for dismissing her so harshly. But instead of seeing a display of contrition, she saw him shaking his head and heard him muttering disgustedly.

"Blue eyes, my ass."

Dave was right: Jake Miller was a man without a motive. He had no financial incentive for murder, just the opposite. With his parents dead, any assets in John's estate would have gone to his son, Josh, not to him. Jake even paid off the Murder House mortgage so Josh would own the property free and clear, and when Josh offered to reimburse him for his expenses, Jake wouldn't hear of it. If anything, John's death cost him money.

Josh had told Regan that his father and uncle were close. She could rule out animosity or jealousy between brothers as a motive.

When she tried to think of a reason for Jake murdering his sister-in-law and the realtor, Roger Commons, she sank deeper into a quagmire of misguided inference. By the time she added Josh Miller's murder to her motiveless bog, she was completely swamped.

There was an added snag to deal with, too, the problem Tom mentioned at dinner, the one that went to opportunity. According to his secretary and to Dave, Jake Miller was away on a business trip when Regan saw him driving by her as quickly as he could in his blue-eyed glory.

Common sense suggested she was mistaken about him being at the Murder House on Monday. A mound of evidence suggested she was off on an improbable tangent yet again. She could almost hear Dave delivering one of his snipes about that: "You know what your problem is, Regan? You don't have any common sense."

She sighed as she maneuvered her car out of the police station parking lot. *Well then, Dave, it's good that I don't. If I did, it might get in my way.*

🏠🏠🏠🏠🏠🏠🏠🏠🏠🏠🏠

"You probably didn't realize you were married to an heiress — not one with a true fortune, but still one with serious assets — who needs advice about investing the money her mother left her to benefit her children."

Tom let out a hearty laugh. "I bet your mother would be more surprised to learn about your financial status than I am; first because she isn't a well-to-do-woman and, more importantly, because she doesn't know she's dead, yet."

"Then we'll have to be very quiet about my inheritance. We wouldn't want her suddenly acquired resources and untimely demise to give her a heart attack, would we?"

"I assume you'll be consulting newly discovered financial advisor Jake Miller for this advice?"

"That's right. I've already made an appointment with him for tomorrow."

"I had a round of golf scheduled for my day off, but I

don't mind cancelling it to come with you," Tom said, sounding every inch the brave martyr.

"You won't have to, I'm meeting with him alone," she could see a slight look of concern flit across his face, "but in a public place, in a restaurant.

"I'll be very busy tomorrow helping a client with Multiple Sclerosis who is buying a get-away condo at Pajaro Dunes. My client tires easily, it seems, and has to take breaks signing all the documents and disclosures involved in the purchase of a beach condo with a history of flooding. I'm being every inch the helpful realtor by arranging for a title company agent to come to his house in Daly City for the signoff.

"Of course I'll want to be present and watch out for his best interests, so I'll only be able to squeeze Mr. Miller into my schedule for a lunch meeting, after and before meeting with my client. He's already agreed to see me. Lunch will be on me since he's being so accommodating."

"You've created quite a lot of back story about your imaginary client."

"You know I'm a bad liar. I'll have enough trouble keeping my nose from growing while I tell Mr. Miller about my made-up inheritance, so my client, his situation, and my extra effort are real, just not current. If Miller asks for more details, I'll have a name and history ready, no blushing or stumbling for me."

Tom raised his eyebrows hopefully, "Or you could look at the preponderance of evidence, decide that you are mistaken about Jake Miller, and skip all this make-believe entirely."

Her silence spoke for her.

"That's not going to happen, though, is it?"

"I have to try this one thing. It's not a matter of pride or thinking I know better than everyone else."

"I know."

"I won't sleep nights if I don't try." Her voice held a note of pleading.

"I know," he said decisively.

"So tell me, is this smile believably friendly?" Regan tried to be lighthearted as she produced an earnest grin for her husband. "Looking like I like the man is going to be the hardest thing by far that I have to fake."

Regan dressed deliberately for her rendezvous. She wanted to look San Francisco professional, but she had special clothing requirements. She selected a huge roomy purse with zippered dividers inside and a handle long enough that it had play when she carried it on her shoulder. Her jacket had to have sleeves short enough to expose the white cuffs on the blouse she wore. After experimenting with three jackets that she thought would work and deciding they didn't, she settled on a loden sweater with three-quarter-length-sleeves. It was dressy enough for The City and guaranteed not to get in her way.

She practiced her moves before she climbed into her car. On the drive, she rehearsed them over and over mentally, like an athlete preparing for a meet. By the time she hit the demands of San Francisco driving, she was ready and confident.

Regan arrived in front of Unicorn, a restaurant less than two blocks from Jake Miller's office, well before one-thirty, the time she had arranged to meet Jake for a late lunch, and began looking for a parking place. She got lucky — very lucky for San Francisco — and found a spot three short blocks and less than ten minutes away; she wouldn't have to run to be punctual or to get to the restaurant in time to select her as yet unknown co-conspirator.

Even after her eyes had adjusted to the light level, the restaurant was dark inside, just like the reviews on Yelp said it would be. After she spotted a past-mid-life server, arranged to be seated in her section, and told the woman what she was up to — with an embellishment she hoped would make the server especially sympathetic to her needs — Regan was ready.

She spotted Jake Miller a few minutes later. He had spoken to the hostess who directed him toward her, but Regan waved anyway — a friendly move designed to help him recognize her in the dim light and to subtly begin preparing him for an animated lunch partner.

Within minutes the busboy had filled their water glasses and their server had mentioned the day's specials, taken their orders, and winked at Regan. The formal titles of Mr. Miller and Mrs. McHenry had been abandoned for Jake and Regan, and she began telling her story of private wealth to her newly cozy financial advisor.

"My mother died last year …"

"I'm sorry for your loss." His words held the genuine note of someone who knew loss himself.

"Thank you. She wasn't a terribly wealthy woman, but she

171

did leave me an inheritance with the instructions that some of the money was to be used to give her grandsons a good start in life. My oldest, Ben, is launched with college behind him and a small house that we helped him buy with some of the money."

"You don't look old enough for ... you and Mr. Kiley must have started your family at a very young age."

His smile struck her as unctuous, but she feigned flattery. "Oh, how nice of you to think so," she matched his performance. "I did start young ... but with my first husband, not with Tom."

He raised his head in a little knowing nod.

"And my youngest, Alex ... well the thing is, Tom takes care of our investments and does a good job with them, but he is terribly conservative. I would like to be more flexible with the money designated for my sons — they are so young and would have time to recover if the market is unkind — and he refuses to understand. I thought you might be able to invest a little more aggressively. In finances — well, in life, too — it's sometimes necessary to take some risks, don't you agree?"

"Absolutely, Regan. Absolutely."

The server brought their food. Regan had the garlic noodles in a spicy red sauce that the restaurant was noted for, and Jake had a giant sea scallop dish. They ate at a leisurely pace and as they did, Jake explained investment options and Regan listened raptly, nodding seriously and murmuring the occasional, "Oh, what a good idea." She bided her time until they had both eaten enough that their meal could end before she allowed her inner klutz to emerge.

"Would you put together a formal proposal with all the excellent options you told me about today and email it to me?"

"I'll be happy to. I still have your contact information on file from when we were involved with the sale of ..."

He hesitated before he said the name, and for a second, Regan doubted everything she believed about Jake Miller.

"... Josh's house."

"Oh no, please don't use that email address. That's for business and I would like to keep this private, just between us. Let me write down the address to use."

She reached down, retrieved the purse she had placed on the floor by her chair, and began to search deep inside it for paper and pen. She scribbled an email address on the paper, and still juggling the gigantic purse in her other hand, reached across the table to hand Jake what she had written.

As her hand drew close to his, the purse escaped her grasp and began a descent to the floor. She snatched her outstretched hand back from his and reached across her remaining noodles in a dramatic attempt to catch the purse before it could upend and dump its contents. Her movement was awkward and too quick. She overturned her plate. The remaining noodles landed in her lap.

She screamed loudly. "Oh no! Look what I've done! What a mess!" She held her hands in the air, a perfect picture of distress and uselessness. "This red sauce will stain. I better try cold water right away."

Regan tossed her purse onto her shoulder and stood up. "Jake, please excuse me."

"Of course."

173

The collision between Regan and the helpful server who came rushing to offer a napkin wasn't hard, but Regan lost her balance. Her purse slid from her shoulder and hit Jake's water glass, which fell over, dumping its contents on the table.

The mouse trap game continued as the server hurriedly threw her napkin at the glass to stop the flow of water; a still seated Jake Miller slid his chair back abruptly to avoid the cascading water, and Regan leaned across him to try an ineffectual and too late move to catch the glass. As she did so, the button on the cuff of her blouse tangled in Jake's hair. She gave a quick twist and tugged it away.

"Ow!" he yelped as she pulled a few hairs from his head.

"I'm so sorry," she apologized as she fled to the lady's room to clean up, abandoning Jake and the server to the watery table.

Once inside the restroom, Regan opened her purse and unzipped the compartment that had remained securely closed during her purse's calamity. She took out a sealed packet that contained a pair of latex gloves, ripped it open, and pulled them on. She removed a small zip-lock plastic baggie, unzipped it, and carefully pulled out the gauze it contained. Next, she turned her attention to the hairs caught in her blouse button. She used great care to disentangle them and carefully capture the root ends in the gauze which she returned to the baggie. Her final step was to zip the baggie and return it to her purse.

As Regan finished with the hairs, her co-conspirator server opened the bathroom door and held out an empty water glass cradled from the bottom in a restaurant napkin. She had a delighted grin on her face.

"I got his glass and I didn't touch the rim. This was fun. I feel like a spy, or an undercover agent or … or someone from Homeland Security," she sputtered gleefully.

Regan readied a second bigger zip-lock bag from her purse and held it open wide. The server gently dropped the glass and napkin into the bag and watched Regan zip it closed. She peeled off her gloves, tossed them in the used hand towel container, and gave the woman a high-five.

"We made quite a team," Regan said. "You did that bump into me as well as if we had rehearsed it for days."

"My pleasure. I can't stand men who won't wear a condom and then won't own up to what they've done. You tell your friend I wish her all the best. I hope the saliva on his glass nails that creep, and the court makes him pay child support for the next eighteen years."

Regan returned to the abandoned Jake Miller after she had wiped her skirt as best as she could and after her heart stopped beating so hard she thought it might leap into her throat. She had pulled it off.

All that remained for her to do was apologize for the way their lunch ended, write her private email address again for Jake, and pay the lunch bill. Had the restaurant lighting been bright enough for him to read the tab, he might have noticed that she left an inordinately large tip.

Instead of driving home directly, Regan stopped at Dave

and Sandy's house. It was after 6:00 and she expected them, or at least him, to be home.

She scooped up the blue-and-white drinks cooler that sat on her car's passenger-side floor and carried it gingerly up the stairs to their front door. There was no need for her care or even for the cooler; once sealed, the samples it contained could be mailed for processing. But to her, the theatrics involved in collecting the samples exacted the added drama of the cooler. She wanted to put a big red bow on the handle, but knew that would be too much; Dave might not appreciate her gift, as it was.

Dave answered the door. A flurry of emotions played across his face when he saw her. There was openness and pleasure at seeing his best friend and guilt when he remembered the harsh words he said the last time he saw her. His eyes conveyed apology, and he started to speak, but then he remembered he thought his words justified, so he didn't.

Regan held the cooler out to him wordlessly.

"What's this?" he quirked his mouth into a lopsided grin. "A present celebrating your retirement? A selection of international beers for me to drink while I think about how peaceful my life will be now that you're out of the detective business?" He licked his lips.

"Not exactly. It's a freshly used water glass and some newly pulled hairs. I went online and looked up the best ways to take surreptitious DNA samples from an unknowing contributor. The saliva on the water glass has an 85% chance of producing a useable sample. The hairs, which do have roots, rate at about a 95% chance. I got both … probably overkill, I know, but …"

"You did what?" His tone was more astonished than cross.

"You said you couldn't compel Jake Miller to give another DNA sample, so I took matters into my own hands."

Dave hadn't taken the cooler from her, and her outstretched arm was growing tired. She dropped the cooler down to her side.

"If you don't want to be involved — or if you think the police shouldn't be — I understand. I can get the DNA run privately. It can be compared after the fact, can't it? I mean, you don't have to run it at the same time as the skeletal DNA, do you?"

"It can be compared later," he said evenly. "You're really serious about this, aren't you? What am I saying? I know you well enough, I should have expected you'd do something like this. Even if this proves your point — and there's no way it's going to since the sample we got didn't, and DNA doesn't lie — there's no authorization, no chain of custody. A match would never fly as evidence."

"I figured it wouldn't, but we'd *know*."

Dave started to reach for the cooler, but changed his mind. He held his hands up defensively in front of his chest.

"No. No, don't give it to me. I better not even know about this. Get it run — I'll give you the names of a couple of reliable labs we use when we're backed up — and then we'll think about how the results are gonna get read and compared.

"I don't know what to do with you, Regan. You are the most stubborn, annoying, clever, dedicated cop-who-doesn't-wear-a-uniform I've ever met. I just hope once this sample doesn't match with the skeleton sample, you'll be able to let your whole dead brother thing go."

177

Two-and-a-half weeks passed and she still hadn't heard anything from the testing lab. For all she knew, the samples weren't even useable. She was prepared for some wait — Dave warned her that her request wouldn't be fast-tracked like it would have been had she represented an official law enforcement agency — but Regan was at the point of regret that she hadn't shipped the DNA samples off to an online paternity testing company of questionable repute that promised, for a mere seventy-nine dollars, that results would be known within ten days.

Not that her clients suffered as the waiting game stretched from days into weeks; she could focus on work well enough from morning until about 11:30, and after the mail delivery which was never later than 12:10. But for that slice of time each day, she paced near the front door like a caged tiger and practically bowled over the postal carrier each time he opened the door at Kiley and Associates to deliver the mail.

The worst day during her wait happened when Jake Miller made a proper and businesslike follow-up call asking if she'd had a chance to review the proposal he had sent and if she had any questions. Her face turned scarlet with the effort to keep her voice even and pleasant as she pleaded laziness and a heavy workload and promised she'd read it over within the next couple of weeks.

Her wait ended on the eighteenth day. The packet came in a manila envelope that was big and thick enough that she knew it contained readouts, not just a "so sorry we couldn't get any results" letter. She grabbed the envelope as soon as she recognized the return address and speed-walked it to Tom's office.

"It's here," she murmured, breathless to the point of feeling lightheaded.

"Open it."

She held the packet in both hands and vibrated it back and forth. "I better not. I'll let Dave open it so there's no question of tampering. Besides, I won't know what any of it means. It will have to be matched to the skeleton's results and read by someone who understands this stuff before it tells us anything."

🏠🏠🏠🏠🏠🏠🏠🏠🏠🏠🏠🏠

Dave appeared in the courtyard of their house three days later just as the sun was setting. He rapped on the glass slider that led into their dining room, but let himself in before either of them had a chance to see who was there. He nodded to Tom who was coming out of the living room; he looked somber when Regan poked her head out of the kitchen.

"Good. You're both here. I have news." He directed them

to their living room. "Let's sit."

He waited in silence for them to both settle on the sofa and took a seat opposite them. Though he was in their house, he was in charge. The oddity of Dave telling them where to be and the fact that it wasn't in the kitchen or out on the back patio where they usually hosted him, made them ill at ease even before he started to speak.

"Neither of you will be happy with what I have to say, but for different reasons. Your DNA sample is a familial match, Regan, just like you thought it would be. Our expert thinks the skeleton is probably John Miller."

"I was right. Isn't that good news?"

"You'd think so." Dave's words seemed upbeat, but what he said didn't match the way he said it.

"Look, maybe it's my fault. I kind of didn't run any of this rematch stuff by the Chief. You — okay, we — have a little history with him. He's not the most flexible thinker I know, and Regan, you have a knack for … disturbing his thought process.

"You shouldn't have done what you did and I shouldn't have passed on the results of your DNA test, but I figured it was better to ask forgiveness than permission, you know, in case he wasn't happy with what you did and that I didn't …" he searched for a good way of explaining what the Chief expected of him, "… control you. He seems to think, because we're friends, I should be able to stop you from meddling like you do." Dave shook his head. "Like that's possible.

"Anyway, when I presented the new results to him, he, well, let's just say he wasn't happy with me. 'Course he couldn't ignore the findings, but rather than climbing on board and thinking for a minute before he spoke, the first thing he did was … was," Dave heaved a great sigh, "he picked up the phone and called Jake Miller.

"You should have heard him. 'So we have this problem, Mr. Miller,' he says. 'A new DNA sample has turned up and the results are inconsistent with the original sample SFPD collected from you about a month ago.' Then the Chief says 'Uh huh, Uh huh' every few seconds for a couple of minutes. Then finally he says, 'I'm sorry you feel that way, sir. You don't need to do that, that's not what I meant to imply,' and hangs up."

Tom began frowning; the creases in his forehead grew deeper as Dave continued.

"The Chief says Miller says he hasn't given another DNA sample and that there must be some mistake. He asked the Chief if he thought SFPD knew what they were doing. Course the Chief had to say he did. Then he asks why the Chief would pay any attention to a new sample that he didn't give — especially not to any authorities — so it couldn't possibly be his, and that he doesn't know what's going on, but that he's not happy to get a phone call that implies he's done something wrong when all he's done is to try and be helpful. Then he says he hopes he doesn't have to talk to his attorney about harassment and incompetence on the part of the Santa Cruz Police Department.

"The Chief is gonna figure it out if he hasn't already — he's not stupid — but he's intimidated right now so he hasn't wrapped his head all the way around the new DNA — regardless of how it was collected — being a match with the deceased. Right now all he sees is the bind he's in because he

181

can't compel another sample without arresting Miller and what you got is useless from a legal perspective."

"What about you, Dave? You believe the skeleton is John Miller, don't you?"

"I'm not stupid or intimidated," he smiled at Regan, "but with Miller stonewalling …" he shrugged. "Right now we got nothin': no motive, no physical evidence, truly nothing to connect Jake Miller with the murders.

"We'd still be after John except for your hair pulling and seeing blue when you should have seen brown — I still don't understand how you did that. But there's no way we can arrest Jake for murder, and if the Chief agrees to have him held on some twenty-four-hour pretext, that guy's gonna lawyer up so fast and hard, we might not be able to get another cheek swab out of him even then.

"The problem is, too, that it doesn't prove he's a killer, even if his new sample matches what Regan got. The most he could get is a lot of suspicious looks from us and a guilty-of-hampering-an-investigation charge. And I bet, between him and his lawyer, they'll have some really nice plausible story for why he did what he did."

Dave squirmed with frustration. "See, right there, SFPD uses the same standard collection procedures we do. They would have checked his ID before they swabbed him, which means we can't figure out how he could have faked the collection. Even obstruction might not fly. He might argue there was a lab error and get the complaint kicked."

Regan was outraged; she ran her list of offenses together in a rapid squeal. "So we know his brother's been dead for almost twenty years, which means Jake killed all those people, and tried to kill Stevie, and wounded Tom and the UCSC Art Director, and there's no way to prove it?"

"Did you listen carefully to what I said or was your mind off whirring the way it does? The way things stand, his guilt isn't proven, Regan. But we can stop wasting resources trying to find John — that's huge — and quietly start focusing on Jake. My guess is he's guilty and that something will turn up or he'll make a slip and we'll get him. I just can't say when."

"He's already had almost twenty years since the first murders and a chance to kill again. Waiting for something to turn up isn't acceptable."

"I told you that you weren't gonna be happy."

"You said I wasn't going to be happy either," Tom said. "You were right about that." He put his arm around Regan protectively and pulled her close. "Miller must know where the new sample came from; he's probably still rubbing his head where Regan pulled out his hair.

"He already tried to kill her the night he took that swing at her and smashed her car windows after she followed him in the woods. If he's killed five people and gotten away with it, he might believe he's invincible and decide to pay her back for all the trouble she's caused him. I don't like this at all. Regan's right, catching him *sometime* isn't acceptable."

"Unless you can come up with a plan to smoke him out, it's the best I can offer."

As they lay in bed that night, Tom assured Regan that she was safe, at least for the time being, since, if he responded at all, Jake Miller would have to think about what to do to Regan for a while before acting. Tom talked a soothing line, but her sleep was disturbed by horrendous nightmares, and Tom, though he wouldn't admit it, spent most of his night sleeping fitfully, awakened by raccoon chirps, cricket sounds, and distant dog barks, normal country sounds not noticed without heightened awareness. He also put the heaviest driver he had in his golf bag within reach next to his side of their bed, hidden from her view by window drapes.

By the next morning, Regan knew, for her own protection and probably Stevie's as well, she better light a fire under Jake Miller. And soon.

Stevie's red Porsche Cayenne was the only vehicle parked at the Beauregard Winery tasting room in Bonny Doon when Regan pulled into the spot next to him. It was just after 11:00, past the tasting room opening hour, but early in the day for random wine tasting, especially given that the winery was three miles up Bonny Doon Road from Highway 1, off the beaten path of casual passing tourists.

She didn't see him inside the tasting room. She should have if he was there because the space was light and open, so she concluded that he must be waiting for her outside behind the building.

Regan spotted him at the edge of a grassy expanse, sitting by a creek where a few tables and chairs were set out in the shade of redwood trees. Stevie was shoeless. The tee-shirt and surfer shorts he wore exposed downy hair on his arms and legs as pale as the hair on his head. He had dragged one of the sturdy wooden chairs to the water's edge and sat with his feet in the coursing rivulet, kicking water skyward occasionally. He looked like a playful baby owl taking a birdbath.

Regan worked her way down the steps from the deck to the lawn and sauntered toward him, looking for the presence of bodyguards as she walked. She saw one man some distance from where Stevie sat. His location might argue he was a Beauregard employee, except he was clearly scanning the area around Stevie and her instead of focusing on winery duties.

It seemed Stevie did indeed have people keeping him safe from a John Miller attack, but John wasn't the one presenting a risk to his safety. She had to tell him that and make him understand he was still at risk, just from a different brother.

The trick was letting Stevie know that John Miller was dead without revealing her suspicions about Jake, because once she told him the truth about the brothers Miller, he would put everything together immediately. She was afraid he wouldn't be constrained by doubt and needing proof like she had been, and unlike the seemingly well-hidden John, Jake's whereabouts were known. Stevie wouldn't have to get John to come to him; he could go to Jake.

If she didn't get Stevie on board by coming up with a workable plan to trap Jake, he might go off on his own and try to avenge his father. She had her work cut out for her, especially since, at the moment, she didn't have a plan.

"Look at this, Regan," he greeted her, beaming in his full baby-toothed glory, holding a wine bottle aloft by its neck. "Your wine is orange."

"My wine?"

"That's why I asked you to come here instead of to my house when you said you wanted to talk. I wanted to show you your wine."

"Stevie, I can't go into a lot of detail, but it's important that you don't ever let Jake Miller get you alone …"

"These grapes are grown in the Regan Vineyard. How sweet is that?"

"I mean it, Stevie. You can't let him offer you private financial counseling or invite him to a private tasting, nothing where the two of you are alone …"

"They use Pinot Grigio grapes from the coldest site in California and let them ferment on their skins in the French style. The wine comes out orange and is called orange wine."

"Stevie, are you listening to me or just babbling about wine?"

"I'm listening. I don't babble. I can think and talk about more than one thing at a time. This is rare stuff, Regan; you gotta taste it."

"Stevie, this is important …"

"You don't have to worry about me hangin' with Uncle Jake. He creeps me out; I get a Darth Vader vibe from him."

"What do you mean? What's a Darth Vader vibe?"

"You know who Darth Vader is, right?"

"Yes."

"And you know he was a guy who went over to the dark side so far he was even willing to kill his own son. Someone who could do that, he'd give off seriously bad vibes, just like Uncle Jake."

Stevie filled a glass with an almost neon orange liquid and

held it up to her. "Everything about it seems wrong but it isn't. It has great balance. You just have to think about the process differently and then it works."

Regan accepted the glass in silence. Stevie was right about more than wine. She swirled her glass in slow counterclockwise circles as a plan formed in her mind. She took a sip. "You see more, understand more, than I give you credit for doing."

He smirked, "Well, yeah."

"I mean it."

Regan took another sip of her wine and decided to go all in.

"Stevie, John Miller didn't kill your father, but I know who did. The police suspect him, at least some of them do, but they have no hard evidence against him. He has to be made to incriminate himself. If you promise — promise — to work with me as partners, I'll tell you who killed your father and what we can do to catch him."

Regan used Stevie's iPad to compose a note. *During the renovation of his house, one of Josh's contractors came across a pink box.* She backed out *a pink box* and substituted *a box tied with a red ribbon. It was hidden in an opening in the sheetrock under a large painting of ...* She hit backspace repeatedly. *hidden box tied with a red ribbon. Josh thought the box belonged to his mother so he opened it and looked at what was inside. After reading the contents, he finally understood what happened at the Murder House all those years ago. He asked me to leave the box in place as part of the house's history — lore — which I've done. But I couldn't resist reading what's in it, too, before I returned it to its hiding place, and since you figure so prominently in its contents, I thought we should talk.* Regan took off the period and added a comma — the letter was supposed to be from Stevie; there should be a Stevie-like offer in it — *over a glass of wine. You don't have to take me up on my offer, but I plan to tell the hidden story in the description of one of my releases.*

Backspace removed *one of my releases* as Regan, as if she were writing an ad promoting a great deal for a limited time only, went for a sense of urgency: *my first release, since it does tie in with my Murder House brand*, she hesitated before going on, *so well.*

She turned the iPad to him, "I think this is what you should send him. What I said hints that evidence exists explaining why Jake killed his brother, at least I hope that's the way Jake will interpret it. Here's the address for his office email."

Stevie read quickly. "Wow. You're really wordy." He typed below her copy:

"Josh gave me the box. Dude, you were bad. The ghosts say we have a lot to talk about."

"That's what I'd say, and in less than 140 characters, even with punctuation, so I could tweet him."

"That would be too public."

"Then I'll text him — I still have his number — but no email. I don't email."

"Get me in there somewhere, too."

Stevie added four words after the third sentence: *Regan says so 2.*

Regan smiled a conspirator's grin, "That works."

Stevie deleted what Regan had written and reached for the send button.

"Wait," she stopped his hand with hers. "If this goes like I think it will, Jake Miller will come after us."

"I'm ready for him."

"I'm not. We need to do some prep work before that," she nodded toward the message, "goes live. And Dave needs to know what we're doing."

"Dave? Your cop friend? No way."

"I understand that you two aren't the best of friends, but the police need to know what we're doing." Regan was glad Dave couldn't hear what she said next, "He's a good interface with them."

"No Dave." Stevie turned away from her abruptly, and with a few taps, sent the message. "And no waiting around, partner. I promised we'd work this together, but I didn't say we'd be slow about it."

17

How would Jake Miller respond to Stevie's provocative text? Would he show up at Stevie's with murderous intent? Would he show up at her house brandishing a machete-sized knife or a bashing rock? Would she and Stevie be safe if they stayed apart, or would he come after them individually?

Regan's mind had raced through those questions repeatedly by the time she reached her office. The most important question, the big question — would their plan work to catch Jake Miller — was crowded out by her more horrific wonderings and worrying.

She already regretted her haste. She should never have told Stevie anything in the spur-of-the-moment way she did; she should have known that she couldn't control him completely. If anything went wrong, if anything happened to him, it would be her fault.

Regan parked hurriedly in the lot behind Kiley and Associates and used the back entrance. She raced down the main corridor so briskly she almost collided with their newest associate. The agent bubbled with enthusiasm as she began talking about her first listing, but Regan dismissed the woman with an uncustomarily curt, "Later, Anne," to continue her rush to Tom's door.

"I've done it now," she blurted out before she saw he wasn't alone.

"Regan, you remember Jake Miller's attorney, Mr. Pedrone, don't you?"

She sighed, "Unfortunately, yes."

The attorney didn't react to her words; he seemed to have an uncanny ability to remain smiling and unflappable in the face of other people's vexation.

"Ahh, Mrs. McHenry. Just the person I wanted to see." He spoke genially, but didn't rise or offer his hand. "My client has instructed me to inquire whether you plan to harass him further or if your propensity for physical assault, insinuation, and name calling has burned itself out.

"If it has, he's willing to forget the friction between the two of you. If not, he feels a talk with the Santa Cruz Police Chief and possibly a restraining order issued against you would be in order as a first step to ending your stalking activities.

"I do sincerely hope you will cease and desist your most offensive behavior because — I assume you may not have realized it — what you've done could lead to criminal proceedings against you."

Regan stared at the attorney defiantly. "Tom, you will make chocolate chip cookies for me when I'm in jail, won't you?"

"I doubt it will be necessary," he winked.

"Make light of my warning if you wish, but realize you have been duly advised to cease and desist."

Mr. Pedrone rose and headed toward the door. "I'll leave you two to consider your next course of action. I can find my way. As I recall from our first meeting, you don't walk your visitors out."

As soon as the attorney was out of earshot, she put her hands to her cheeks. "I may be more serious about those cookies than you think. Let me tell you what I did — what Stevie and I did — now."

She was the last one in the office, putting on her jacket, picking up her purse, and ready to leave, when she got a real phone call from Stevie. He started talking as soon as she answered.

"Regan, game on. It's like you thought, Uncle Jake wants to know what's in the box. He has a guilty conscience all right. He's coming to my house tonight."

"Tonight?" Her stomach tightened. She hoped their accusatory message would force Jake Miller's hand, but not so soon. She hadn't even told Dave about her scheme yet.

"Yeah, at 8 o'clock. He said he had to come by tonight because he has a busy week. He asked if you'll be here, too. What he really means is he's freaked out about what's in the box and about what we know. You think he's gonna try something tonight, you know, like try to kill us or something?"

Stevie sounded delighted at the prospect of an imminent attempt on their lives. 8 o'clock. Regan tucked her headset against her shoulder, took her cell phone out of her purse, and checked the time, 6:40. Things were happening too fast; she needed more time to think, to plan.

Stevie overrode her thoughts as he so often did. "I told Uncle Jake that I got rid of my security guards."

Regan felt a wave of panic, "You didn't, though, did you?"

"Yeah, I did. They were only to protect me from a John Miller surprise attack. Now that I know who to look out for and when he's coming, I don't need them."

"Stevie, that doesn't seem like a good idea."

"This game is between Uncle Jake and me now; I don't need them around giving me an unfair advantage ..."

It was Regan's turn to cut him off. "This isn't a computer game where you can walk away if your avatar gets killed, Stevie. Jake Miller is dangerous. He doesn't deserve a level playing field."

"I never said I was going to play fair, just one on one. You worry too much. Are you coming at 8:00?"

"I'll be there. Soon." She didn't say it out loud, *and hopefully with Dave.*

"Okay. See ya."

Regan dialed the first four digits of Dave's office number before she realized that he'd probably have left for home by then and changed her mind. She hit speed dial for his cell phone and tapped her fingers nervously on her desk as his phone rang repeatedly.

He answered on the fourth ring. "Hey, Regan, I was just about to call your house. Give me a minute to turn the news off and grab a beer."

"Dave?" She said his name with urgency, but he didn't hear her; he had put his phone down. She waited for what seemed like an hour before he spoke again.

"You and Tom both there? I've got news you two should know."

"Tom has a listing appointment. I have news for you, too. Tell me yours quickly before I tell you mine."

"Jake Miller couldn't have done the original murders; he didn't kill the Miller woman or your little weirdo's dad."

She shook her head like she might have done after spending the night in a strange bed and awakened not knowing where she was. "What? What do you mean?"

"After our little talk, I pulled the whole Murder House file — you've got me callin' it that now — to read. I wanted to be completely familiar with everything in it; I figured I might come up with something that could help us make Jake slip up. I started at the start, which is always a good idea, and figured, given his family connection, an initial interview of Jake Miller would be in the first few pages of notes, but it wasn't. In fact, I couldn't find any notes about an interview with him until a week after the killings.

"Turns out, he wasn't interviewed right away because he'd been out of town, back East, and gotten into a car accident. The guy spent the day of the murders in an emergency room at Brigham and Women's Hospital in Boston. So no way he killed his sister-in-law and Roger Commons."

"But Dave," Regan said incredulously, "he took the bait. He's acting like a man with a guilty conscience. That's my news. He's coming to Stevie's tonight."

She could hear the frustration in his voice, "I start at the start with you, why do you always start in the middle of what you're talking about with me?"

"Stevie and I sent Miller a message. We said we found

194

something hidden that connected him to what happened at the Murder House. Now he wants to meet us at Stevie's tonight to see what we have."

"And what do you have?"

Regan had a mental image of Dave with deep lines in his brow and between his eyebrows as he tried to follow what she was saying. "Nothing. We made it up; we were trying to smoke him out."

"Look, Regan, I verified the hospital records. He couldn't have been out here slashing and bashing at the time of the first killings. Yeah, he was in town when Josh and your realtor friend bought it, but we've always believed whoever did the second murders did the first because of the way the bodies were placed. They had to be put that way by someone with intimate knowledge of the first murders. Your Jake Miller isn't that killer. So now we've not only got no motive for him killing everybody in sight, we have conclusive proof he couldn't have."

"But the DNA. John Miller is the body in the woods and Jake tried to make it seem like he wasn't."

"I've been thinking about that. Maybe he didn't. Maybe there really was some lab error with the SFPD sample and he genuinely thought his brother was still alive. You said yourself Miller's sending a note and letting himself be seen didn't fit with the killer's MO. Maybe all he did was keep up his efforts to stop the Butler kid from using the Miller family tragedy to push wine. If you think about it, especially from Jake Miller's point of view, what your little ghoul wants to do is pretty cruel."

"Then why won't he give a new DNA sample and finally

settle things?"

"Maybe he's ornery; maybe he's had enough. Why do you keep trying to make something out of so little when nobody else does?

"It's like you think you see a zebra hiding out in the middle of a herd of horses and insist on lassoing every one of them and dragging them to a corral hoping you'll see the zebra again. Maybe what you thought was a zebra was just a horse with striped markings. I'm asking you to open your eyes and see the evidence when it's irrefutable."

"Did, that smarmy attorney that Jake uses have a talk with you, too? Is that why you've changed your mind?"

"What are you talkin' about now, Regan?"

"Pedrone. That's his name. He said if I didn't leave Jake Miller alone, he'd speak with the Police Chief and get a restraining order against me."

"No one told me to change my mind about anything. I'm just looking at what's in black and white. I bet your message to Miller is what caused his attorney to get riled up."

"Stevie sent him a text before the attorney visit, but there wasn't enough time between when he did and when Mr. Pedrone turned up at Kiley and Associates for Jake's attorney to have driven down from San Francisco where he works. Jake Miller's attorney came because of what I did in San Francisco. What Stevie and I did today didn't precipitate his courtesy call.

"You should know that I didn't want Stevie to send the message when he did ... I wanted to talk to you first."

"That's swell of you. What did you tell Miller you have?"

"We said that Stevie has a box that Miller's nephew Josh

gave him. Stevie said the ghosts and I thought we should tell him what was inside it."

"Scheesh." Regan heard a long sigh followed by soft chuckles coming over her headset. "See, now if I got a text like that, I'd turn up, too, even if I didn't have a guilty conscience. Who can resist ghost directives?"

"This isn't funny, Dave."

"Debatable. You and your little buddy, knock yourselves out at your meeting with Miller. You can have lots of candles for light and maybe have your pal's bodyguards wear sheets with holes cut in them so they can see; it wouldn't look good if ghosts were bumping into one another.

"Then, after you two hatch your little plan and have your fun, why don't you try to explain to Miller how you're really not trying to give him more ammunition to get a restraining order."

"They'll be no sheeted bodyguards. Stevie sent them home. He says they were only around to prevent a surprise attack from John Miller and that now that he thinks Jake killed his father, he welcomes taking him on one-on-one."

"You told ghoul-boy that Jake Miller killed his dad?"

"Sort of … yes, I did."

"Well then, you better un-tell him before Miller shows up or things could get messy, couldn't they? What time did you say Miller was due?"

"I didn't, but 8 o'clock."

"Then you better get a move on; it's already almost 7:00, so you don't have much time then, do you?"

She tried Stevie's land line and cell phone with Dave's admonition still ringing in her ears, dialing repeatedly until she hit Empire Grade Road and her cell service did its Bonny Doon shutdown. Stevie answered neither phone.

Regan didn't take time pulling into her garage. She yanked off her jacket before she was through the front door and kicked off her heels as she rushed toward her bedroom closet — the heels would have to live where they landed in the hall until she returned home.

She exchanged her business clothing for jeans and a sweater with similar speed. She slipped on one flat shoe; the second flat wouldn't cooperate. She hopped back toward the door holding the shoe by its heel and maneuvering her foot into it as she went.

Her speed exceeded the residential limit, and more importantly the speed limit of safe driving, as she returned to Empire Grade Road. She hit her brakes hard when she rounded a bend and narrowly missed hitting the smallest of a trio of dogs arrayed across the road on their individual leashes which were out on an innocent evening walk with their owner. She beeped her horn.

The dog walker yelled, "Slow down," and shook his fist in the air — a fence to be mended when she had time.

Ice Cream Grade was the most direct route across the capital letter A that the main roads in Bonny Doon formed, but it was also windy, with washed-out spots where it narrowed to a single one-car-at-a-time lane. She didn't hesitate when she reached the shortcut, though, turning off Empire Grade Road to plunge down onto the tortuous route because it would bring her to Bonny Doon Road in the shortest amount of time.

Regan parked in front of Stevie's house at 7:40, having

broken many speed records to get there so early. There was no sign of Jake Miller.

"Made it," she whispered to herself.

She was up the steps and landings in a flash, pounding loudly on Stevie's front door. It creaked when he opened it for her — still creaked, she noted.

Stevie seemed calm, but his cheeks were flushed pink with excitement, which was incongruous amid his otherwise uniformly pale features.

"You ready?" His lips parted around baby-sized teeth that, as unlikely as it seemed, looked sinister.

"We have to call everything off!" Regan exclaimed. "Jake Miller was in a hospital room in Boston when your father was killed. I was mistaken; he didn't murder your father."

Stevie blinked rapidly, "Are you sure?"

"One-hundred-percent sure."

"Then who?"

"We're back to the start; we don't know."

"But I've … I made a prop." His disappointment was palpable as he let her in and closed the door behind her.

"You're really sure?" he asked again as they moved toward the living room.

A box — Stevie's handiwork — about the size of a shoe box but half as tall was sitting on a low table in front of his living room sofa. It was a perfect size for their plan; it could have held a myriad of unnamed secrets. He had taken some time with it; it was white and had a narrow red ribbon tied once around its narrowest side to form a shoelace bow, but it was doctored, made to look slightly dirty, as if it had been subjected to years in a less-than tidy hideaway.

They had barely reached the living room when a strong rap sounded against the front door. Stevie picked up the box and started to slide it under his sofa out of sight.

Regan's thoughts rushed. In his angry frame of mind and after sending his attorney to intimidate her, Jake Miller's response to their message should have been fury and legal action. Instead he had hastily driven down from The City ...

"Leave it," Regan instructed him on impulse. "You're right. He did come. Something prompted him to drive all the way here from San Francisco. He may not be a murderer, but he's got a guilty conscience. Let's stick to our plan for a while and see if we can get him to tell us why that is."

She shrugged, "I'm going to be doing a lot of apologizing again after tonight anyway; one more affront isn't going to make him any angrier at me than he is already."

Regan took a seat facing the entry as Stevie once again maneuvered the groaning door open. He wordlessly invited Jake Miller inside and motioned him toward the living room with a wave of his hand.

"I hope you don't mind that I'm early," Jake said looking from Regan to Stevie. He shifted his weight from foot to foot, the same artificial smile on his face that she had seen in San Francisco. "Traffic was light from The City; I made good time."

"It's Okay. We're ready for you," Stevie answered calmly, but the pink in his cheeks flared even brighter.

Jake remained standing and wasted no time in getting to the point of his visit. "I understand you have something you think I need to see, something Josh gave you? When did he do that?"

Regan thought she heard anger in Jake's voice.

Stevie ignored much of what Jake asked as he launched into the language he and Regan had devised at the Beauregard Winery. "It's something interesting," he said, 'in the box."

Stevie pointed down at his creation. Jake's eyes lingered on Stevie's face for a long time before they slowly moved to follow his direction.

Regan's real estate job had trained her to read body language clues. When he saw the box, Jake's blue eyes narrowed and his mouth twitched ever so slightly. To her, he looked like a man trying to mask the effect of a body blow.

According to their plan, Regan's opening line was supposed to knock him off balance with an accusation. She had rehearsed saying, "We believe what's in the box explains why you killed your brother John, his wife, and Stevie's father."

She changed her line slightly: "We believe what's in the box explains why your brother killed his wife and Stevie's father."

She hadn't accused him of anything, but Jake seemed to cease breathing. Regan didn't ask, she stated: "You know what's in the box, don't you."

Regan had learned most people, especially when they're nervous, can't stand the cessation of words. Regan, counting on Jake to fill the void her silence created, waited quietly after she spoke.

"You said I was bad. You've read the letters. I know how it must look …"

Letters!

Regan hadn't planned for Stevie's reaction to quiet tension or his propensity to interrupt. He stopped Jake with an exuberant bit of improvisation.

"So, it looks like my father was Josh's father, too, and that means Josh was my half-brother, so you're kind of my uncle." Stevie rushed at his new relation and wrapped his arms around him. "Uncle Jake."

Jake remained rigid, his arms stiffly down at his sides. Gradually though, he relaxed and a calculating glower spread across his face. He returned Stevie's hug.

"I guess we have more in common than I realized."

Jake was unnerved before Stevie's welcome-to-the-family outburst, Regan was sure of it. He had revealed that he thought the box contained letters. He was about to say more about them, but Stevie stopped him — saved him — before he did. Jake might not be a murderer, but he did have a guilty conscience. What had he been about to say?

Regan tried to regain control of the conversation, tried to take it back to where Jake felt vulnerable. "You're right, Mr. Miller, we think you were bad ..."

"Well, yes, but you can't blame me for my oversight. Until now I didn't know how Stevie and I were connected because of Josh."

He and Stevie could be related; Jake was even better at shutting down her line of questioning than Stevie was.

"But now that I understand our connection, of course, I'll be sure to rectify that. You'll find I am a very steadfast uncle."

Jake sounded like a reformed Scrooge talking to his oppressed employee, Bob Cratchit. He sat down on Stevie's sofa, took a pair of glasses out of his coat pocket, and put them on the table in front of him.

"I'd like to read the letters in the box now, if you don't mind."

No one spoke. Jake had called their bluff. Stevie looked at Regan with wide-eyed alarm. They had been caged and Jake had pushed the key to their cage into the lock, ready to turn it.

"There aren't any letters in that box, are there?" he asked.

Regan's mind flew as she searched for a way to answer him. *Letters.* Jake came because he thought they had a box of letters. *Old letters implying guilt.* Regan did her best to keep breathing evenly. Not ordinary letters: *love letters!* Stevie had accidentally hit on what the imaginary letters were; he just got the lovers wrong.

"You're right, Mr. Miller. The box is empty but only because we emptied it. Stevie didn't read the letters. Once he recognized what they were, he — well he thought it would be upsetting to read something so private between Mrs. Miller and his father — so he gave them to me to read.

"I know what the letters say, Mr. Miller, who they're from, and what that means."

Stevie opened his mouth to speak. Regan shot him a look he couldn't misinterpret. His mouth snapped shut.

"We haven't told anyone else about them. Once I understood what we had, we took them out of the box and rewrapped them in a more protective covering. Letters like that — such beautiful letters — should be carefully preserved. We're keeping them tucked away like Mrs. Miller did. We think it's what she would have wanted."

"Where are they? Where did June keep them? Where did

you put them?"

Jake spoke too quickly, too eagerly. Her guess had been correct.

"We put them back in a place not involved in Josh's remodeling. They're part of the house's structure again, only this time they're protected in case the roof leaks. It doesn't matter where they are, though, since they're safe. I know that's what you'd want: for them to be safe from judgmental eyes."

Stevie's head whipped back and forth between them like he was watching a tennis match.

"What do you want, Mrs. McHenry?"

"Nothing. Nothing much. Your acceptance, perhaps. Stevie wants to use them — oh, don't worry, only their existence and sentiment, no names — in his narrative for his first release. He didn't want you to be caught by surprise. Consider this a courtesy notice."

"Yeah, Uncle Jake, I wanted to let you know before I go public. You don't mind, do you? It's not like you have anything to do with the letters. You don't have a guilty conscience or anything, right?"

"No. Yes. Thank you."

"Oh, Mr. Miller, there is one thing you could do for me." Regan smiled benignly as she spoke, "You could call off your attorney."

"Consider it done," Jake replied with more self-possession than Regan expected, but he still sounded like a man beset.

He picked up his glasses and pocketed them. He got to his feet slowly, never taking his eyes off of Stevie as he rose. "I'll let myself out."

Stevie's front door squealed in complaint as Jake jerked it open rapidly and disappeared through it into the dark of a moonless night. He gave the heavy door a pull to close it, but didn't stop to try again when it failed to latch. The door moaned desolately and reopened a few inches, enough that they were able to hear his car door slam and his wheels spin on Stevie's driveway as he gunned his engine.

If it was possible for an inanimate vehicle to convey emotion, as he drove off Regan thought his car sounded enraged.

"He'll be back to search my house, won't he?" a grinning Stevie asked. "He wants the letters my father wrote to June Miller; the letters we made up."

"Yes, he does."

Stevie thought the letters were written by his father; he hadn't guessed what she had. Regan prayed his ignorance could protect him, but she worried it wouldn't.

Jake Miller may not have killed Stevie's father and June Miller, but Regan was almost certain that Jake's recent impersonation of his brother John was done to cover murder, possibly even three murders.

"Please, recall your bodyguards right now, before I leave."

"You think he'll be back tonight?"

"I don't know what he'll do and I won't know until I figure out for sure what he's already done. I think I know, but I need to talk to your mother to be sure. Would you give me her phone number?"

"My mother? Why?"

"I have to talk with her about your father."

Stevie frowned. "Okay," he said hesitantly. "Sure. We can

call her right now."

"Just give me her number. I need to talk to her woman to woman, no sons, no husbands around. And you — call your bodyguards right now."

"I don't call bodyguards. I text them."

Regan watched as he typed his text. She felt better when he sent the message. Hard as she had tried to make Jake Miller think only she knew his secret, Jake's hard looks at Stevie worried her; she wasn't sure she had succeeded.

Even if she had, if her suspicions were correct, Stevie was still a witness to what she had said to Jake. If anything happened to her, Stevie would figure out what the implied letters meant; he might on his own, anyway. Stevie was as much a danger to Jake Miller as she was; it was just a matter of time before he realized that.

Myra Butler opened the door to her cheery house high up on Pau Hana Drive in the hills above Soquel and invited Regan inside.

"Did you find us on your first try?" she asked. "Most people think it's tricky to get here, even following GPS directions, because of the way the road splits."

"I've been a realtor long enough to know every road in the county and I sold a house a little farther up your street some years ago, so I'm familiar with the road's quirks."

There was an awkward silence once the niceties of their greetings were said.

"Thank you for letting me come by."

"You were so secretive when you asked if we could meet, and then when you mentioned my son's safety might be involved ... what is it you want to talk to me about?"

Instead of answering, Regan glanced around the house's open floor plan, making sure they were alone.

Myra picked up on Regan's inquisitiveness. "My husband's home, but he's out in his studio. He's trying his hand at writing — a police procedural mystery, he says —

now that he's retired. He goes out there carrying a cup of coffee in the morning and doesn't come back inside until his stomach tells him it's lunchtime." She raised her hand and looked at her watch. "We should have a good hour and a half to talk without being disturbed — that is what you said you wanted to do, isn't it?"

"Look, I'm sorry if I've been melodramatic. I had a first marriage and sons, too. I don't talk candidly about their father or the end of the marriage in front of them and I don't necessarily do that in front of my husband, either. I have questions to ask that I thought you might feel more comfortable answering in private."

"What do you want to know and how does it involve Stevie?" Myra clasped her arms around herself as if she felt a chill.

"I knew Stevie's father. I know Roger had a reputation. Did you find out he was having an affair with June Miller, the woman he was murdered with? Is that why you were divorcing him?"

"How do you know I was divorcing …? You do get right to the point, don't you? No, he wasn't having an affair with June Miller."

"Had he been involved with her in the past?"

"He was in high school," Myra said dismissively. "He took her to the junior prom, but they were over before the senior prom."

"Nothing after that?"

"No."

"Are you sure?"

"Yes, I'm sure. He came home laughing about running

into his old high school girlfriend when he listed that house. What are you suggesting?"

"The word in the real estate community is that Mrs. Miller's husband caught them in a compromising position and that's why he killed them."

"That was the favorite police theory at the time, too." Myra studied her hands. "Look, everything you heard about Roger's behavior was true — until our son was born. Fatherhood hit him with a righteous bolt — he changed. He grew up. I think he learned his womanizing ways from his father, and when he had a son, he said he didn't want to pass along ... Roger said he wanted to be a good role model. He didn't want his son raised like he had been. Roger promised to be faithful and, by then, he was. You said you were divorced?"

"Yes."

"In your marriage, was there a moment when you knew it was broken beyond repair?"

"Yes," Regan said. "I remember it well. I was at the park with my sons ..." her voice trailed off.

Myra nodded. "Then you understand. Roger turned over a new leaf, but the problem was, long before he did, I had to shut down my feelings for him — and I certainly loved him early on — to survive. By the time he recommitted to me, I'd reached a point where I no longer loved him.

"It was right about then that I reconnected with Frank. Ironic, isn't it, that once Roger was faithful, I was the one who was cheating."

"Does Stevie know?"

"Of course not. What happened between Frank and me,

it's not something you tell your child about. We just let it seem like we got together during the murder investigation. Frank took some heat for that at work because police aren't supposed to get involved with a murder victim's family members during an active investigation, even if they're not part of the investigating team. But I was a grieving widow and everyone liked Frank. Truth be told, I think his fellow officers thought our getting together was romantic — cops are a romantic bunch for all their toughness, you know — and were mostly supportive.

"Frank has been a wonderful father to Stevie. He's always treated him like he was his own son; they love one another like father and son. What Stevie thinks he knows about Roger has made his relationship with Frank easier."

"I think you're underestimating both your son and your husband. Stevie won't love your husband any less when he knows the truth about his father, and Francis has proven for years how he feels about Stevie."

Myra bristled. "You got an invitation today because you said my son was in danger. How does what's in my past relate to my son's safety?"

"I told Stevie that John Miller didn't kill his father, that it was Miller's brother Jake who was the murderer."

"Why would you think that? The police are sure John Miller …"

"I made a mistake. The police are right: Jake didn't kill Roger. But John didn't do the latest round of killings, and he didn't make an attempt on Stevie's life at the media event. He couldn't have, because his body has been found. He's been dead for many years, but whoever tried to shoot Stevie is still out there. You have to convince your son to keep his bodyguards because he could still be at risk.

"There's something else, Myra. Stevie seems to believe Josh Miller was his half-brother, that Roger fathered them both. Stevie relished the idea of avenging his father's death. I'm afraid if he thinks his father was having an affair with June Miller and that Josh was his half-brother, he'll add Josh's murderer to his revenge list and confront whomever he believes killed Josh. If he's mistaken about who that is, he could harm an innocent person.

"And if he's right and challenges a killer, well, Stevie may be brilliant in his own way, but he's no match for a real murderer. That's why you have to tell him what you just told me."

Regan sat her gift on the counter and filled in her name badge. She hadn't told Dave she was coming, but she had checked — he was in his office.

"You know he's moved?" the desk officer asked.

"Yes. I've been to his new office."

"I bet you have," the officer smirked. She had seen Regan before — even chased her once, ready to draw her weapon before Dave intervened — and knew about their connection. The officer handed her a visitor badge and buzzed the door open for her.

Regan held the potted plant in front of her as she walked into Dave's office.

"What's that?"

"It's an office warming gift."

"It's a pink plant."

"It's a Pink Zebra Earth Star plant, my way of saying I'm sorry if I cause trouble, because you're right: I do think I see zebras."

Dave's face cracked with a satisfied smile.

"And to let you know I've seen another one."

His smile dissolved.

"Sit." He pointed to an interview chair across from his desk. "Talk."

She put the pink zebra plant on his desk and sat as instructed.

"I got to Stevie's before Jake Miller did and told him we needed to change our plans because of what you said: that Jake couldn't have killed his father, but Jake arrived before we had a chance to rethink what we were going to say. Stevie had made this box ..."

Dave rolled his eyes.

"... you should have seen Miller's reaction to it. He stammered and got pale, so I ... I interrogated him just like I've seen police do on TV ..."

Dave moaned dramatically.

"... and let him tell us what he thought was inside it."

"Which was what?"

"Love letters. Even though Stevie almost ruined everything when he tromped on my interrogation and said the letters were between his father and Mrs. Miller, I was able to recover by saying Stevie hadn't read them, only I had.

"I've spoken with Stevie's mother — just to make sure her

dead husband wasn't involved with June Miller — so I know I'm right. Jake was the one she was having the affair with, probably for years. From the way he reacted, it looks like Jake wrote love letters to June and that he's afraid she kept them. He's worried about his letters and wants them back.

"Are you willing to look for zebras with me?" Regan put up her hand holding her thumb and index finger close together, "Just for a tiny minute, because I'm getting pretty scared of one of them named Jake."

"You did bring me a plant — it's a pink plant — but it's an interesting one, at least. Go on, not that I could stop you."

"I came up with a scenario: Jake and June started having an affair which they kept from John, at least until June got pregnant. I have this source, a woman who knew the Millers well. According to my source, June confessed her infidelity to her husband and promised him the affair was over, but said she couldn't swear the child she carried was his. According to this same source, John was a wonderful man who promised to treat the child as his own, regardless.

"Supposedly, June never told John who her paramour was — I mean she couldn't if it was Jake, could she?" Regan shook her head, her eyes open wide.

"Since they were related, that would mean they'd have to see one another regularly, though, at family gatherings and all."

"And all." Dave was mocking, but he was interested.

"If they still had feelings for one another, that must have been awful for them. At some point, I think they resumed their affair. John probably suspected his wife was being unfaithful again, but still didn't know with whom. That's why he decided to sell the house and get his wife far away from temptation.

"Then, like the police theorized, John came home early one day and found Roger Commons, the realtor he hired to sell the house, laughing with his wife. They went to high school together; they even dated in high school. Can't you imagine the two of them reminiscing innocently about old times when John, already suspicious of his wife, walked in?"

"I'll leave the imagining to your fevered brain."

Dave's comment didn't slow Regan's unfolding of her theory.

"So John, thinking he had discovered who his wife's lover was, snapped and killed them, just like the police think."

"You're not saying much that we don't know or suspect — except for your source. You want to give me a name?"

"Hang on, I will in a minute. I think June either told John about his brother with her dying breath or John found the letters."

"I thought you made up the letters."

"We made up the box, not the contents. The letters must have been written or Jake wouldn't have been so concerned we had them." She fluttered a hand. "It doesn't matter. Assume John found out about the affair somehow and confronted Jake. Don't you think they'd fight if that happened? Jake said he was the bigger and stronger brother. He could have overpowered John and — it might have been an accident — killed him during the confrontation.

"However John wound up dead, Jake buried him at the Murder House, and then, to cover up what he had done, acted like his brother was still alive and in hiding."

Regan leaned back in her seat and raised her eyebrows. "Works, doesn't it?"

"It explains John's being dead in the woods all these years, I'll give you that. I don't understand why he would bury his brother and fake his disappearance, though. With your scenario, Jake could have come forward and claimed self-defense."

Regan only needed a few seconds to come up with an answer. "John could have told him he knew about the letters, maybe even said he had them. If they turned up, a judge or a jury might not think John's death was an accident or justified. Better to let his brother vanish.

"His nephew Josh complicates things, too. I think Jake cared about him very much. How could he tell him what he had done?"

"I kinda like your scenario. You could be right."

"You're not arguing with me?"

"John had to get planted by someone. We agree that Jake seems like a pretty good planter candidate. Your letters idea isn't a bad explanation for why he might have taken up rustic body farming."

"There could be more."

"Oh yeah? Like what?"

"You said Jake couldn't have killed June and Roger Commons — and I agree — but Jake could have been the one who took a shot at Stevie during the media event. It makes sense if he was trying to make it seem like his brother was still alive and annoyed at what Stevie was doing with the Murder House."

"Nice of you to agree Jake isn't a mass killer since,

215

remember: hospital, Boston, perfect alibi, but you really figure he'd take pot shots to keep his illusion going?"

"I do. I think he's the person in the woods who attacked me, too. He may have been planning to dig up his brother's body and rebury it somewhere else to make sure it wasn't discovered when Stevie had the trees taken down around the burial site before he started planting grapes.

"Dave, I think I was right all along about Jake being a murderer, though just of three people not five. He not only killed his brother, I believe he killed Josh and Inez, as well."

"You think Miller killed the nephew you just said he couldn't bring himself to tell what he'd done to his father? And why would he want to kill your realtor friend?"

"When I first met Josh, he told me he had seen, if not his mother being killed, at least the aftermath, but blocked it out of his mind for years. He said, living in the Murder House, he was beginning to remember things — memories long buried — and to see things. He said he remembered seeing his father covered in blood. Suppose he started remembering more. Who knows what Josh saw, and if he blocked out his mother's death, maybe he blocked out later things, too, like John confronting Jake or his uncle killing his father.

"Jake may have felt that to protect himself, he had to silence his nephew. And poor Inez, well she would have been another realtor in the wrong place at the wrong time, just like Roger Commons was."

"Makes sense."

"Wow. I didn't expect you to agree so easily." It took her a few moments before she spoke. "You don't agree, do you? You're letting me run on and you're not buying anything I've said. Not for a minute."

"Guilty as charged," he grinned. "Regan, you have a real thing about Jake Miller. His brother … maybe … probably; I told you we're looking into that. But you keep trying to moosh him into a guilty jar and make him responsible for everything bad that's ever happened in Bonny Doon. The thing is, the harder you try to push, the less likely he is to fit, and the closer your jar gets to breaking wide open.

"Whoa, there it goes right now!" He put his lips together, filled his cheeks with air, and blew, "Phoosh! Tell you what, though, if your favorite bad guy comes back looking for imaginary letters, you let me know."

Dave picked up the zebra plant and moved it from his desk to the top of a filing cabinet in the back corner of his office.

"Thanks for the plant. I kind of like it, especially the sentiment, but I can't have a pink plant as the first thing my fellow officers see when they stop by — bad for my tough-guy reputation.

"You still scared of your Jake-zebra?"

"Why would I be? According to you, I have nothing to worry about from him."

"So what I have to tell you is too long for a text," Stevie said as he slouched in a chair in Regan's office. "That's why I'm here." He pursed his lips together until they resembled a beak. "My parents had me over for dinner last night. We had a long talk."

"And you're all comfortable with ..."

"I never really thought I had a brother. Well maybe I did, sort of, but I don't anymore. I already changed my narrative."

"The ghost in the woods paid me a visit — paid my house a visit — last night while I was at my parents and tossed the attic."

"What?" You mean Jake came back ..."

"Not according to a neighbor. According to him, it was the ghost in the woods. The neighbors put together this petition to get me to take down the crystal cairn. They say it's attracting the ghost. How stupid is that? I'm not doing it. It's my land, and my cairn, and my ghost, and they can't tell me what to do."

The pink in his cheeks began ever so slightly as he spoke and increased in hue the further he got into his rant.

"Could you start over and tell me what your neighbor said?"

Stevie derided the man, "He's one of the bigger neighborhood idiots."

"Stevie."

"He said he was taking his dog for a walk. I asked him why he was walking his dog after dark — I think he was spying; he's a nosey old guy."

"Stevie." The second time she said his name, Regan's voice had a sharp edge to it.

"So maybe he did get home from work late," Stevie smirked. "Anyway, he said he noticed a light in the woods. He said it started near the cairn and moved steadily toward my house. He said his dog started barking and the light disappeared, but that he made his dog be quiet and he held still, and after a few minutes the light came back and went to my house.

"Then he said he could see the light inside my house moving higher up until it finally got all the way to the attic. He said he could see it shining through that little air vent in the peak.

"When I checked, I saw the insulation had been pulled down from between the rafters in the attic. He thinks we hid the letters under the insulation, right?"

Regan nodded. "That's why I said what I did to Jake about the letters being safe from roof leaks. I figured he had ample opportunity to search the house when it was derelict and probably had, but that an empty attic was one place he might not have looked at carefully, so he would believe we had hidden them there."

"My ghost pulled all of the insulation down. Oooh," Stevie chuckled, "you don't think there really were letters in the attic and that he found them, do you? How cool would that be?"

"More ironic than cool," Regan said. "It sounds like Jake must have a favorite parking spot away from the house and moves through the wood using a flashlight."

"Well yeah! But my idiot neighbor thought he saw a ghost. I am going to light the cairn from inside and see how long it takes him and the others to figure out they're seeing basic modern technology and not a ghost."

"You said the ghost, the light, came when you were gone. Do you think he was watching your house?"

"Who knows. I got a text from my mom inviting me for dinner, so I was gone when he came by. He might have been watching my house and seen me leave."

"Stevie, this has gotten serious. If Jake was brazen enough to break into your house and casual enough to leave evidence he had — not to mention that you may be right about his search — that makes us — both you and me — loose ends. He'll be coming after us next; we have to ask for police protection."

"Isn't that the whole point of everything so far, to get him to come after us? I told you I'm ready for him."

"Stevie, he's killed three people. You're — we're — in over our heads."

He shook his head vigorously. "Look out for yourself; I know what I'm doing."

Regan called Dave as soon as Stevie, undissuadable, left her office. His phone went to answering.

"Dave, you said to let you know if Jake Miller came back.

He searched Stevie's attic last night while Stevie was having dinner with his parents. Stevie's full of confidence and itching for a confrontation; I'm worried — terrified — that such a clash won't end well. Call when you get this, will you?"

She hadn't put enough urgency into her message. Regan debated calling Dave again with a revised plea when she remembered the capable looking man she'd seen at the Beauregard Winery discreetly tending to Stevie's welfare. That memory and bright afternoon sun reassured her.

She peered out her office window. It was odd how much daylight mattered. During the day, help felt close at hand; after nightfall, the world could become a different place, full of night terrors and danger. The sun was hours from setting and she and Stevie would be safe for the time being, even if Dave was slow to respond to her message.

Tom poked his head into her office. "I'm heading home. I want to get a head start on marinating some steaks for dinner tonight since I promised George he could have anything he wanted for his birthday celebration and that's what he ordered. Are you coming home sooner or later?"

"I should be about half an hour behind you. I'll swing by Kelly's Bakery and pick up his cake on my way."

"Sounds like a plan." His head disappeared as quickly as it had appeared.

She started to call after him to tell him about Jake's break in, but decided against it; Dave was the man she needed on this job, not Tom.

A couple of minutes later her phone rang for the third time

since she'd tried Dave. Surely this was him and not another client call. "Dave?" she asked as she answered.

"No, Mrs. McHenry. This is Jake Miller. Stevie asked me to call you."

Her lips parted and she inhaled sharply, audibly.

"I'm here with him right now. He thinks you should join us. We'll expect you within twenty minutes or he thinks things could get ugly. Oh, and Mrs. McHenry, there's no need for you to contact the police about our little get-together. I have to tell you, if you're not alone, that will create difficulties, as well."

Regan continued to hold the phone to her ear for several seconds after it went dead. She finally returned the phone to its cradle and reached for her cell phone with its preprogrammed speed dial to Dave's office. Her first try produced the same result she'd had earlier: Dave's answering message.

She hit speed dial for Dave's cell phone. When it also went to answering mode, Regan slammed her phone to her desk. She worked to gain control of her panic before the outgoing message ended and she was allowed to speak.

"Dave, Jake Miller is at Stevie's. He's threatening harm if I don't get there immediately or if I tell you what's happening. He says no police, but you've got to help us!" She fought to bring her voice down from the hysterical pitch it had reached. "Dave, Dave, please be there, please pick up. Dave?"

Regan disconnected and called Tom. His phone rang; he didn't answer. He must have already reached the Bonny Doon dead zone on his way home, but since he had only left minutes before, he wouldn't get home for many more minutes. She hung up and called home.

Had she reached him, Tom would have done everything possible to keep her from going to the Murder House. And she certainly didn't want to go, but she had no choice.

"Tom, get Dave." Regan spit out tight bursts of information on their answering machine. "I'm on my way to Stevie's. Jake Miller is there. Tell Dave he has Stevie. He said no police, but Dave needs to bring the cavalry."

Her voice quivered as she finished her message. "I love you. I'll always love you."

20

Regan sped for the entire eleven miles between her office and the turn off of Highway 1 at Bonny Doon Road. She didn't go five miles over the fifty-five mile per hour limit; she drove a dangerous fifteen to twenty miles over it. Not a single CHP or sheriff's patrol car materialized. "Where are they when you want to be caught?" she raged.

Her mind raced for the entire journey: what should she do once she reached Stevie's? Should she goad Jake with the obvious: that she hadn't obeyed his demand, and she had called the police? Should she try intimidating him with the fact that people knew she was going to where he held Stevie?

If any harm comes to either of us, you're as good as convicted. Should she say, convicted of murder? Maybe not. He had already killed — don't remind him that with us, he has nothing more to lose.

Stevie's red Porsche Cayenne was parked at the bottom of the steps and landings leading to the front door. A late model black Mercedes was parked next to it — a well-off investment advisor's car if ever there was one — dark, sleek, and menacing. Regan pulled her car past both vehicles and stopped next to Stevie's SUV, a subconscious message of solidarity in parking.

For a moment she toyed with the idea that since her Prius was a silent runner, Jake Miller had no idea she'd arrived. Perhaps she could somehow sneak up on him and overpower him using the element of surprise. Her wishful thinking ended as the Murder House door groaned open before she reached the final brick step.

Jake Miller stepped back from the door, gravely making way for her to enter. As she passed him, she noted he was more than a little tense; his forehead was covered with perspiration. He held a gun down at his side in an unthreatening pose. The mere presence of a gun in his hand was enough of a threat however; there was no need for him to raise it or aim it at her to make her shiver.

Although Jake was her immediate focus, as soon as she crossed the threshold, the gloom inside the house began competing for her attention. She felt exposed in the light of the open door behind her as the sensation of an almost spectral shadow enveloped her. Her eyes struggled with the transition from bright sunshine outside to oppressive darkness inside and she blinked rapidly, hoping that act would help her see more clearly sooner.

"Stevie is waiting for us in the living room." Jake spoke with such solemnity that she feared she was about to find Stevie's body. He leaned against the heavy door, and as it groaned closed, Regan fought to see Stevie in the dark.

At first she could only make out his outline, but as her eyes began adjusting, she saw that he was sitting very upright on a chair brought in from the dining room, motionless, with his hands in his lap and his head bowed.

She hurried toward him, reached out her hand, and touched his shoulder.

"Stevie?"

He raised his head and producing a subdued baby-toothed smile. "Hi, Regan. Sorry about how things worked out."

He was alive — unharmed for the moment — but hobbled at the bare ankles below his shorts and wound at the wrists with cables and cords ripped from various electronic devices that were upended, smashed, or in disarray among overturned living room furnishings. Had Stevie's bodyguard put up a fight on Stevie's behalf? Was his body in another room?

"He got my gun."

Regan forced herself to take a deep breath and to look around with care. Now that her eyes had adjusted to the low light and she could see well, she needed to fully understand her situation if she was going to do anything about it.

Although the ceilings were high and the room had many windows, the Murder House living room was never the brightest of interior spaces. Heavy drapes framed the windows, but they were normally wide open to encourage the penetration of outside light. Today they all were pulled together tightly. The same was true of the dining room drapes; and the kitchen, visible through the dining room, which was normally sun-filled, was dark as well. Heavy blankets covered the kitchen windows in haphazard ways, hastily nailed in place, Regan surmised.

No light filtered down the long staircase from the hall and bedrooms above; if anything, the stairs looked like they entered a dark cave and terminated out of view. Similar care must have been taken upstairs to produce such depressing murkiness.

Stevie noticed her observations. "Uncle Jake told you not to talk to the police, but he doesn't trust you." He aimed his head and his words at Jake and taunted, "He doesn't like SWAT teams and their snipers."

Regan took a quick look at Jake, afraid he might react to Stevie's words and tone with violence, but Jake remained impassive.

She could hear her heart thudding in her chest, but Regan reached deep inside trying to, if not find calm, at least project it. She had to keep their captor calm, too, and she knew that Stevie, with his ability to be brash and abrasive, wouldn't help their situation.

As she watched him, Jake raised his downcast eyes and, like she had done, surveyed the room around him. "So many lives have been lost here; this place is such a perfect cage," he said.

She had to make it seem like she had as much control over what happened next as Jake Miller did. Tom must have picked up her message by now — perhaps Dave had as well. If she could get Jake talking, if she could negotiate something, anything, she might buy enough time for help to come.

"I came like you asked me to. What is it that you want, Mr. Miller?"

He didn't look at Regan; his gaze slowly turned toward Stevie. "This nightmare, it isn't what I want," he sounded forlorn and desperate.

Stevie's shout was so sudden and forceful that it startled

both Regan and Jake. "It's time, Uncle Jake! It's time for you to pay. Tell us what you did!"

Jake threw up his empty hand like he was defending his face from an attack, but the hand holding the gun remained at his side.

Stevie seethed, "Look up, Jake, look at the stairs. June wants to talk to you. She wants you to confess."

At the sound of her name, Jake's mouth fell open, he tilted his head back and looked up toward the darkest part of the house.

A light glowed at the top of the stairs, faintly at first but soon with more brightness. As it intensified, it slowly descended the stairs and the center of the glow took on a human likeness. The staircase was visible through her, but the visage of a young dark-haired woman dressed in red became clear. She reached out her arms imploringly as she spoke.

"Jake, Jake, what have you done?"

"June," Jake whispered her name.

"Jake, why have you hurt me so? You killed your brother and then your own child. Josh was your son, not John's."

The scream that rose from Jake's throat didn't seem human. It sounded as if a chasm that reached to hell had opened, letting all the tortured souls suffering there cry out at once through him.

"No, June, no!" he shrieked. Then his words became almost imperceptible and his body convulsed in sobs. "You know how much I love you. I killed John — I couldn't let him live after he killed you — but I could never hurt Josh; I could never hurt your son." He dropped to his knees. As he collapsed, the gun he was holding struck the ground and bounced along the floor, moving closer to Stevie.

Regan had been transfixed by June's image and Jake's reaction to it. She hadn't noticed Stevie working his way out of his awkwardly tied cords. His feet were still bound, but once Jake's weapon was loose, he stretched out his now-free hands, and with a deep knee bend, sprung like a bird taking flight. His arms were rigid and his hands fully extended toward the wayward gun.

June disappeared abruptly to reform as a soft glow at the top of the stairs and began her descent again while uttering the same words she had spoken before: "Jake, Jake, what have you done? Jake, why have you hurt me so? You killed your bother and then your own child …"

Stevie's fingertips reached the gun's barrel and he drew it toward him, bobbling it along the floor until it was under his body.

"… Josh was your son, not John's."

Jake was like a man emerging from a trance. He no longer hung his head remorsefully; he completely understood the past and saw his future. As June finished her accusation a second time, faded, and began to reappear at the top of the steps, Jake became full of fury.

"You," he panted. "You did this!" he yelled as he dove toward Stevie with his left hand reaching toward Stevie's eyes like a claw.

Stevie rolled to his side, pulled the gun out from under him, and fired at his attacker. Jake made no sound. His head crashed to the floor and he lay still.

Stevie sat up, and with a smile on his face, slowly turned the gun toward Regan.

The front door seemed to explode off its hinges and collapse into the foyer. Men sporting protective vests swarmed through the opening with weapons drawn and aimed in various directions. A window in the dining room tinkled to the floor behind its covering and three similarly clad men pushed their way through the drapes and repeated the action taking place at the front of the house.

Two armed and vested policemen charged up the stairway through June, who was once again accusing Jake of murdering his own son.

Loud voices began echoing "clear" from all directions. Regan was pulled to her feet — her knees must have buckled; she didn't remember dropping to the floor during the preceding moments — and asked, "Are you OK, ma'am?" by a towering young officer.

Stevie remained in his sitting position. In the still dark room, his cheeks glowed pink as if luminous embers were embedded just under his skin. He was pulled to his feet by officers on either side of him and asked the same question.

"Yeah, I'm good." Stevie looked over his shoulder at Jake's prostrate figure. "He was going to kill us — Regan and me — and lay us out like the other owners and realtors. He told me that was what he was going to do, but I stopped him."

Stevie's tiny teeth clamped down on his lower lip as the officer on his right carefully removed the weapon Stevie still held tightly in his hand.

An unresponsive Jake was turned on his back. The officer kneeling over him with his fingers pressed to Jake's neck yelled, "He's alive," and uttered an order for an ambulance into the handset he produced.

As if to confirm his life-force was still present, Jake groaned and opened his eyes.

The police had pulled some drapes open and in the increased daylight, Regan could see the intense blueness of Jakes eyes. He rolled his head toward her and tried to speak. His mouth repeated the same movements several times before he was able to form words.

"Tell June," he seemed to plead with Regan, "I ... didn't ..." His eyes fluttered and closed.

Regan looked at Stevie. He was a grinning raptor, his baby-toothed smile full and his eyes glistening with the aftermath of blood-pumping exhilaration. He reached into one of the pockets of his cargo-shorts, took a second to find what his fingers sought, and said, "June, shut down."

June collapsed into herself and her words ended with "your own." Then she flickered and faded away completely.

"Holograms are so cool," Stevie stated triumphantly to no one in particular.

Tom arrived before the ambulance got there, and Dave came in a couple of minutes before it left carrying the unconscious Jake Miller. Though the intensity of the experience exhausted her as if it had unfolded over hours, Regan had only been present for about five minutes of drama. With ten minutes of questioning, she outlined what happened and answered all the questions posed by the officer in charge. As she did, she frequently glanced at Stevie who was being similarly debriefed. Each time their eyes met, Stevie's lips curled up into a tiny, constrained grin.

"Can I take her home now?" Tom asked after the officer's

questions became repetitive.

"In a bit," the officer responded.

Dave intervened. "Let her go. We're friends. I'll talk to her first thing tomorrow morning, or the way it works, she'll want to talk to me and have me tell her it looks like she was right about Jake Miller all along."

The officer in charge waved his hand. "Sure. Go then."

Tom put his arm around Regan's shoulders and hustled her out the door before anyone could change their mind.

"I'll drive, and fast."

Tom opened his passenger door and gently guided her into his car. She'd been through a lot and, although she was physically unharmed, she was withdrawn and distracted; he expected what had happened to emotionally overwhelm her at any moment.

When he was settled in his seat, he reached across her and secured the seat belt she had forgotten to fasten and then maneuvered down Stevie's driveway and out onto the road, quickly, as he had promised.

"I left George and the other guests grilling their own steaks," Tom tried some light-hearted chat to help her keep her equilibrium. "Now you can help me stop shirking my hosting duties."

Regan turned and leaned toward her husband with tears rimming her eyes, "His plan didn't work the way he expected, but if it had, he was going to kill both of us."

Tom pulled his car over to the shoulder and turned off the ignition. He reached for his wife, pulled her as close as he could, given the central console in his car, and stroked her hair as he spoke.

"It's over, sweetheart. You're safe, and Stevie's safe, and Jake Miller, well from the looks of him, he's not going to be able to do any more harm for a very long time."

"That's just it: I was wrong about him. I was wrong about both of them. It wasn't Jake who was going to kill Stevie and me. It was Stevie who was going to do the killing."

By 8:00 the next morning when Dave showed up at their house bearing three tall cups filled with brew from the Santa Cruz Coffee Roasting Company, Regan couldn't have given a coherent description of what became of their dinner guests. Whatever happened to them, they were tidy in their leaving. There was no mess to clean up. The only sign that people had been at their house at all was a dishwasher full of implements arranged differently than normal and a lack of the chocolate chip cookie dough they kept in their freezer for baking at open houses.

The people who were invited to help their friend George celebrate his birthday might have quietly eaten dinner or they might have left shortly after Regan and Tom returned home. Regan remembered George handing her a full glass of wine and insisting she drink it, but not much else until she was sitting cross-legged on the sofa in their bedroom telling Tom what she had witnessed at Stevie's house.

"I had no idea how bad you two were going to need this," Dave said, as he sat the coffee holder on their kitchen counter and pulled out two of the cups. "I know what a disaster Regan looks like without her war paint on, but Tom, this morning you look more wrecked than she does."

Tom rubbed the stubble on his face. "That's because, while we were both up all night, she wasn't worried about her like I was. Like I still am."

"Well, Tom, if Regan's right about Jake Miller being our killer, there's nothing to worry about. He's still alive, but barely, from what I hear. Even if he makes it, all Regan's gonna have to do is testify in a nice safe courtroom and that guy will never see the outside of a jail again, not after doing three murders."

"One murder, Dave, according to Regan. It's unclear to her whether or not it was premeditated." Tom sipped his coffee.

"It must be too early for my ears to be working. Could you repeat what you said, because I think I just heard you say Regan let Jake Miller off the hook for a couple of homicides. Is that what you said, Tom?"

"You heard right."

Dave watched as Regan heaped sugar into her cup and stirred it around. "Regan?"

"You know I'm not fond of Jake Miller, and he is a killer — he admitted to killing his brother for what he had done to June — but with what could turn out to be his last words, he denied responsibility for Josh's death. If he didn't kill Josh, he didn't kill Inez, so one murder only."

"Hey, I've been at work since 6:00. I've read the reports from last night; nowhere in those reports did you say Miller's last words were 'I didn't kill Josh.'"

"He didn't say it like that, not so clearly, but he started to.

235

He reiterated what he said earlier when he thought June was accusing him of killing his own son. And the way he threw himself at Stevie ..." Regan changed gears abruptly as she stopped stirring, "Dave, is there something wrong with Jake's right arm, is it broken?"

"What?" Dave screwed up his face, "What does his right arm have to do with him saying he didn't kill Josh and — yeah, it would have to work that way — and your realtor friend?"

"Jake held a gun in his right hand the whole time I was there, but he never moved his right arm: not when he was startled, not when he tried to defend himself, and not when he tried to attack Stevie. Something must have been wrong with it because it didn't work.

"If I put myself back in the Murder House and watch what was happening objectively, Jake seemed to be deferring to Stevie the whole time."

"Wasn't your little ghoul tied up — like you stated last night — while Miller was armed and free to roam around?"

"That's what it looked like ... except ..."

"This is why we were up all night," Tom interjected.

"... except I'm not sure that's what was happening. Has Jake regained consciousness? Has anyone asked him to tell his version of what happened last night?"

"As far as I know he made it through surgery, but his wounds are life-threatening; he's not up to any kind of interrogation yet."

"Dave, why aren't you telling me how foolish I sound? I know what I think seems implausible. I expected by now you'd be all over me, laughing at me and my theory."

"Yeah, well, maybe I should be. Going off on your idea about John being dead because of Jake Miller having blue eyes instead of brown eyes is still nuts. But, it turned out you were right, and — if you breathe a word of this to anyone on the force, we won't be friends anymore — I'm pretty proud of how you got Miller's DNA to prove it.

"The thing is, sometimes you are right." Dave sighed loudly, "And sometimes you and I agree even though no one else sees things like we do, at least not at first."

"Dave? Do you think I'm right? Do you think Jake was doing what Stevie told him to do instead of the other way around?" Regan was incredulous.

"There's a lot to consider … if you asked that question even a few days ago, my answer would be different … it took me a while. Oh, what the heck. Probably," he nodded his head. "This case is about as messy as it gets. You got old murders, and it looks like the guy who committed them has gotten away with it for twenty years. You got new murders that were staged like the old ones, which means they had to be done by someone with knowledge of how the first murders went down, someone like the original bad guy. But then it looks like he got himself killed twenty years ago, too. And then there was the San Francisco detour unwinding everything we thought we knew."

Dave looked from Regan to Tom; they both had quizzical expressions.

"Okay. So after you came up with that new DNA, the Chief was in a tizzy. He sent me to The City to poke around and see what went wrong with SFPD's original collection. He told me to do everything on the down-low and not make any waves. Well, I'm nothing if not the picture of discretion. When I looked into how the results of 'ole Jake's DNA were so wrong, guess what I found out?"

Dave answered his own question before either of them could. "I found out how he duped them."

"Jake faked his DNA?" Tom asked. "I didn't think that could be done."

Regan put her hands on her hips, "You knew Jake faked the test results and didn't tell me?"

"Sorry. Did I fail to mention that to you before?" Dave grinned mischievously. "It wasn't that hard for him to do as it turns out. He brought a friend with him — a stand-up buddy who was gonna drive him to the airport as soon as Jake gave his sample. Well, once Jake's ID was verified and his fingerprints were logged in, they both suddenly started feeling bad — both supposedly had been on a fishing trip to Baja a few days before and picked up a little case of Montezuma's Revenge — and left the room in a hurry before Jake could get swabbed.

"By the time Jake came back, the day shift had ended, and there was a new sample collector on duty. Pretty easy for his friend to say he was Jake and for Jake to say he was the friend. Turns out there are online sites that tell guys how to beat DNA collection for paternity suits and that's one of the techniques they recommend. All it takes for it to work is timing, a good buddy, and some ballsy behavior. Besides, since Jake wasn't a suspect for anything and he was trying to clear his brother, SFPD expected him to be honest.

"Bottom line is once we knew the Jaker was a faker, it was like when we knew John was our John Doe: it changed the way the investigation proceeded. 'Ole Jake looked good for killing his brother and burying him in the woods — like you thought — otherwise why would he have gone to all that trouble to cover up who the skeleton really was?

"Lots of questions got answered once we figured Jake was our guy. He probably was the one who smashed your car. Jake-in-the-woods with a shovel getting ready to move his brother's body before escrow closed made sense.

"Then after John's body was found, Jake taking potshots at Stevie makes some sense, too, if you think about it."

"I did think about it," Regan mustered indignation. "I suggested that to you. You disagreed with me."

"It's so much fun to do, 'cause you get so darn worked up," he laughed. "But when you make a good point, I listen to you even if I don't act like I do. If he was the shooter, Jake Miller disrupted Stevie's big donation announcements, and maybe that's all he wanted to do — figured he could scare the Butler kid off — but if he had killed your little weirdo, so much the better; Butler's death would have been pinned on John's already guilty shoulders and that would have been the end of that. No donations. No facial reconstructions. No identifying our John Doe in the woods.

"You even gave me that idea about why Jake might have killed his nephew and your realtor friend, too — you remember — that the nephew was starting to dredge up old memories. You said Josh remembered seeing his father all bloody the day he murdered Josh's mother and Roger Commons. Maybe Josh witnessed a later murder as well.

"Jake Miller took his nephew in right away. Suppose John came to Jake's place and that's where he was killed. Josh might have seen his uncle killing his father and suppressed it like he did the first killings. Little kid, lots of trauma — I could see that happening.

"At one point, I had it worked out that maybe John unloaded details of what he had done before Jake killed him and that's how he knew what to do to make the new murders look like the originals. I passed all that info along to the Chief who thought I was a genius until he remembered that Jake Miller was away on business at the time of the second murders.

"Now me, I'm a skeptic about alibis, especially tidy ones from a guy who knows how to mess with his DNA sample. I always want backup proof when it's a buddy alibiing my favorite suspect, or in this case, his well-paid and devoted professional assistant, who either didn't know where good 'ole Jake was or lied about him getting back from his business trip sooner than he said he did — which we know he did since you saw him and his baby-blues in an old Buick when he wasn't supposed to be back.

"This time they were right, though, he was out of town, so 'bye 'bye solution. That meant Jake really couldn't have done the new murders, either, so there had to be another way for the person who did them to know about the old murders.

"The thing is, since the first murders, we've gone digital. All the photos of the crime scene, the notes taken, the interviews with witnesses — everything — has been computerized ..."

Regan and Tom's voices were perfectly synchronized: "Stevie could have hacked the files."

"That's what I think." Dave took a dramatic pause and

struggled to suppress a smile before delivering his next words, "So like I said before when you were wrong about his parents, the Butler did it. That's why I hustled you out last night. I thought we should talk before I tossed my new idea in the Chief's direction. Besides, I sure didn't want us chatting about him in front of the little ghoul, not if he is a killer.

"There's a small issue remaining that needs to be worked out: another alibi. Your Stevie has a friend who said they were playing video games at his place all day when Josh and Inez bought it. I figure his pal could be just like Jake's SFPD buddy, but the Chief might not see it like that; I want some hard evidence before I go to him.

"So, Tom, you used to program. Can someone tell if our files have been compromised by looking at them?"

"You'd need a computer forensics team and a lot of time to know for sure, but I can tell you it could be done — in fact it has been done: I read that a twenty something is in federal prison for hacking into a police system — but the hacker would have to be darn good."

"Stevie's that good," Regan said.

"Short of this slow forensics team, how do we find out for sure if Butler messed with our files?"

"Suppose I ask him," Regan said.

"I'm being serious here, Regan."

"So am I."

"Okay, seriously, then. You ask him. What makes you think he'll tell you?"

"There's one thing I know for sure about Stevie: he likes an audience. If we're right, Stevie has just pulled off a spectacular production, one he's been working on for months

— maybe longer. He's twenty-one. For him, the time spent on this is a large percentage of his life; he must be dying to tell someone about what he's accomplished."

"I thought you said your little ghoul was smart. You think he'd be willing to confess and face jail time or worse, just to get some recognition? I don't think so."

"If Jake Miller dies, if Stevie thinks there's no future trial, no real police investigation going forward because everyone thinks Jake's the murderer, he'll want to tell someone how he did it. After last night, the way Stevie looked at me, he already knows I suspect him — at least I'm pretty sure he does. He'll have nothing to lose."

"Of course, if he tells you, he'll have to kill you after he confesses," Tom's pronouncement lacked any humor. "Didn't you think he would have killed you last night if the police didn't arrive when they did? No, Sweetheart, this plan of yours is a nonstarter."

"He can't hurt me now that everyone thinks Jake is guilty; he doesn't have another suspect to blame if I die. Oh, I don't doubt he'll try to come up with a way for me to have an accident, but Stevie's not going to act impulsively. He's a planner — look at all the steps he had to take to get to this point. It will take him some time to figure out an elegant solution for my demise."

"Ya know," Dave mused, "I think you're right. Except for your realtor friend — he had to take her out because she caught him with blood on his hands," Dave's eyebrows shot up, "probably literally — Butler's not an impulse killer."

Dave chewed his lower lip, nodding as he did, "Yeah, he'd want to make sure he has a nice little alibi ready for when he does Regan to death; that's the way he works, all right."

"I'm glad you're so certain," Tom was irate. "Would you feel so confident if it was Sandy in Regan's place?"

"Regan is already at risk. If her little weirdo did what she thinks — what we think — he did and has any inkling that she suspects him, at some point, he's gonna want to tidy up. Better to push him and control his timing."

Tom was unhappiness personified. He couldn't argue with Dave's reasoning and Regan seemed beyond being persuaded, but he gave it a final try.

"Sweetheart, one of the things I most love about you is your Crusader Rabbit heart; it's also the trait you have that causes me the most anguish. If you have to make me miserable, couldn't you do it by flirting with buff twenty-eight-year-old men at parties, or criticizing me in front of my friends, instead of putting yourself at risk by trying to get justice for those you think aren't getting it?

"Even if you get Stevie to admit he's been behind everything, what good will that do?"

"It's like Dave says: the focus of the investigation will change. It will help if we know how he thinks."

Tom shook his head. "Nothing will be different than if Dave took his theory to his superiors right now. Your standing there nodding your agreement with him won't make his case any stronger, neither will you explaining why Stevie did what he did.

"What worries me most is that you and Dave think Stevie's got to plod along looking for a new way to handle inconvenient you. You think the kid's bright, exceptional even; he may be a quicker study than you give him credit for being."

"Stevie's a linear thinker — that's why he does so well with math and science — but I saw how flustered he got when we had to change plans quickly after I told him Jake couldn't have killed his father. Stevie's not fast on his feet. Things didn't work out like he thought they would last night. He'll have to rethink what he does now; that'll take him more than an overnight."

"Unless he has already been formulating a plan with a different ending. Sweetheart, how do you know he hasn't been working on a contingency plan?"

Regan's lips parted, but she didn't have any reassuring words for him.

Dave let Tom's concerns play out, then he ignored them. "Okay, so I'm going to work now. I'll arrange for an officer to give our suspect a call and let him know Jake Miller didn't make it. If he contacts you and you can, get him talking — just keep your distance."

🏠🏠🏠🏠🏠🏠🏠🏠🏠🏠🏠

The phone in Regan's home office rang about an hour later. Stevie launched questions at her as soon as she answered it.

"Did they call you? Uncle Jake died."

She tried to assess his frame of mind from the inflection he used. It was difficult over the phone — she relied heavily on body language when she tried to read her clients — but she thought she detected anxiety in his voice.

244

"Dave told me."

"Oh yeah, your cop friend."

Their conversation faltered into silence. She had practiced asking Stevie to meet her at the Beauregard Winery where they had plotted the trap for Jake Miller. It was a private enough place where he should feel comfortable talking, but public enough that Tom wouldn't worry about her too much.

"Stevie, after what happened …"

"Regan, I'm kind of freaked out. I had to get out of my house. I'm at the beach — I thought I'd feel better — but it's not working. Do you believe in ghosts?"

"What?"

"Can I come by your house?"

"No!" she yelped.

"Why not?" He sounded like a nine-year-old being told he couldn't play any more video games.

Stevie sounded so innocent — and so wretched — that she had to remind herself of what she thought he had done.

She imagined hosting a meeting of The Ladies of Bonny Doon, a stalwart group of local women who promoted charitable work in the community, in order to sound convincing. "Because I have a house full of ladies coming for lunch and we won't be able to talk."

"What time will they leave? I could come over then."

"I have to go to work after that. You could come by my office," she tested.

"I don't like your office that much; too many realtors."

"I could meet you on West Cliff Drive at 3:00. Do you know where the Wee Hoose is?" Regan named the often painted and photographed Santa Cruz landmark, the one surviving dwelling on the ocean side of the road that hadn't been reclaimed by the sea in its relentless march inland.

"Yeah."

"Let's say at the bench closest to the Wee Hoose in the lighthouse direction. There's a bench that sits well off the sidewalk. We can have a nice quiet talk."

"Okay. See ya."

Regan closed her eyes and dropped her shoulders as she took a deep breath and released it. Tom appeared in the office doorway.

"I was listening. You're going to meet him, aren't you?"

She nodded, "In public, though, where casual enjoyers of our community's amenities can keep us in full view."

"You won't mind if I'm one of them, will you? I understand there have been a number of humpback sightings this week. I've been meaning to set up a scope and see what I can see … in disguise, or course. You want me to be a guy with a full beard and a floppy hat or a fat lady in a dress?"

22

Stevie was already sitting on the bench when Tom parked three houses back from West Cliff Drive on an intersecting street. He picked the spot because it gave him a good view of the rendezvous bench.

"I'm glad I don't have to fight with a bushy beard or a bunch of stubble-hiding foundation," Regan said before she pecked his cheek with a little departing kiss.

She let herself out of the car and walked slowly toward Stevie. The bench she picked was set high off the ground; his feet didn't quite touch the sand below it. His head was bent down and he was engrossed with his iPad. He looked like a child dressed for the beach in flip flops and baggy shorts. Had she not been there last night, Regan would never have believed he was anything more.

"Stevie."

He startled at his name, looked up, and blinked, owlish behind his round dark-framed glasses. "So do you believe in ghosts?" he asked hastily as she sat down next to him.

"Probably not. But my mother swore her favorite uncle stood at the foot of her bed the night he died three thousand miles away and said goodbye; with that kind of upbringing, I won't say absolutely not."

"Yeah, well I don't."

He looked paler than usual, if that was possible, and his face told a tale of deep tiredness, like he'd had a tougher night than she had.

"Is that what you wanted to talk about: the existence of ghosts?"

He didn't answer her question.

"I've been working on a new game. It's called Revenge Quest. I want to tell you about it. In my game there are demons that invade your world and kill people you love. It's war; your goal is to avenge their deaths and take down demons until you make the world a safe place again. In my game the demons look like everyone else at first except they have a red tattoo on the palm of their right hand."

He rolled out the details of his game quickly, speaking like he always did: at a pace that discouraged interruptions.

"There's balance in the game; I like things to be in balance. You have to balance the speed of your attack with making sure you only kill demons. The demons are always trying to make you kill humans, and you can't help it, you will kill a few."

Regan wasn't aware of flinching, but she must have as she thought of Josh and Inez, because Stevie stopped his exposition briefly. When he spoke again, it was more thoughtfully.

"You're allowed some mistakes; innocent people always get killed in wars. You have to be careful though, because what makes this game different is the way it's scored. You get positive points that make you a stronger demon slayer whenever you kill one of them and even more points if you get a demon to admit what he is before he dies, but you get negative points when you kill humans."

Regan rested her elbow on the bench back and cupped her hand over her mouth. Stevie's perspective was clear; she had no words to say.

"The demons you've killed can feed off your negative points and turn into demonic ghosts who come after you — you yourself, not just people you love. It doesn't matter that the demons deserved to die, they can still haunt you, and they're a lot harder to kill the second time.

"Wait till you see the graphics I have in mind for them once they turn into demonic ghosts; that little stunt I did with June's hologram is nothing compared to what I have planned."

"Your game ... is it real?"

"I got the idea from my life. John Miller was the first demon and my dad was the first human he killed."

"And Jake, where does he fit into your game?"

"Uncle Jake? He's a demon, too; you already knew that, didn't you?"

"Are you sure about him? He admitted to killing his brother. If John was a demon, doesn't that make Jake a fighter like you?"

"No, it doesn't. He's the most powerful demon of all. He set up John to start killing. Jake and June — what they did — the lies they lived — that's what caused my dad's death. John only finished what they started."

"Will you answer a question for me without filtering it

through your game?"

"I like my game."

"Stevie."

"Maybe."

"Were you going to kill me last night?"

He smiled in reaction to what she asked; the same smile she'd seen the night before: his expression was coy, and it hid a hint of something dark underneath. "What happened to you last night was completely up to Uncle Jake, up to the demon.

"When he came to me yesterday, he thought I didn't know what he was. He was calm, like an executioner. He sat down with me and said he was sorry about what he had to do, but that he was an avenger like he had been for June — demons will say things like that, they'll try to make you lose focus.

"His plan was that we'd be alone and he could take me out, but I was ready for him. He had a gun with him, but he hesitated. I had my gun, too, in my pocket. I said you have to play the game fast; I drew first. He didn't put up much of a fight even when I hurt him. He's past sixty, you know, old for a demon."

"Why did he call me? Did he want me there, too?"

"No," Stevie shook his head, "Oh no. He said the game should just be between us; he was afraid if you were there, you'd get hurt. I told him as long as he played by the rules and confessed, you'd be safe, and he would live.

"I'm the one who wanted you with me. When he confessed, you'd be a witness. Game over."

"And if he changed his mind and didn't confess?"

Stevie wagged his head. "Then there would be a battle. When I won it, you'd still be a witness; game still over."

"Neither of those things happened though, did they?"

"Not exactly. He thought he would be confessing to killing his brother. He freaked when he realized he had to confess to causing Josh's death, too."

"The battle I saw wasn't fair, was it?"

Stevie's expression was amused for the first time since they began talking. "The gun you saw Jake holding might have been empty."

"But you shot him with that gun," Regan frowned.

"Did I? Maybe Uncle Jake's gun just looked like the one I used." He patted a bulging pocket in his surfer shorts, "See, Regan? You didn't notice this pocket before, did you? Pockets are almost as good as holograms for messing with people, especially when there's a lot going on and no one's thinking about what might be in them."

"You didn't give Jake a real chance, did you? After you shot him, he wasn't supposed to have any final words."

Stevie shrugged.

"I am a witness, Stevie, but to Jake Miller saying he could never hurt Josh. He knew Josh was one of the innocent people you killed in your war, didn't he? That's the real reason he came after you."

Stevie's nostrils flared and his eyes became mere slits behind his round glasses. "Josh might have been an innocent victim, but his death was necessary. Absolutely necessary. His father killed my father, so it's perfect symmetry if a son kills a son for revenge."

His breathing was rapid and he pressed his hand against his chest.

"At least, that's the way it should work in Revenge Quest.

I should be getting balance points, getting stronger, but there's a bug in the game that I haven't worked out yet, and Josh's death hurts me as much as my father's did."

"Stevie, you have to turn yourself in …"

"What do you mean? All I've done is fight demons in a game."

"Stevie, your stepdad could help …"

"He wouldn't understand and he wouldn't help. He was a cop all his life. When I was little, I begged him to catch the bad guy who killed my father, but he never did. He said there were rules. He'd have no appreciation of my game."

"Then we can talk to your mom."

"My mom told me about how she was doing the same thing as June. In my game, that would make her a minor demon."

"Your mom told me about your stepdad and her, too. What your mom did — I think it makes her very human. Stevie, let's go see her. Let her help you."

He shook his head. "She couldn't. That's why I wanted to talk to you. You tried to stop Uncle Jake." He smiled up at her. "You're a real demon fighter at heart like I am. You understand about rules having to be broken; you're about the only person I know who might get my whole game plan."

He pressed on his chest again; a soft moan escaped his lips.

Sitting where they were in a public place and with Tom yards away watching, Regan didn't fear Stevie. He seemed more like a damaged child than a killer. She slid closer to him. "Are you okay?"

"I told you how the game works. Uncle Jake fed on my

negative points. His ghost is stronger now; strong enough to hurt me."

Stevie's story raced forward, "Right before dawn this morning, he and June — their demonic ghosts — came to my bed. I sleep in the room where June died, but I'm not like my neighbors: I've never seen her ghost before." He chuckled softly, "That's probably because I don't believe — didn't believe — her ghost was real.

"It was strange because Jake looked the same as ever, not maniacal like he looks in my game. He didn't even seem angry, but he sat on my chest, holding me down until I couldn't breathe; I still hurt today because of what he did. What June did was worse, though. She didn't have any power like Jake did, but she just kept wailing at me about Josh until it felt like my heart was shattering.

"So, was I going to kill you in the game last night? No way. You're a human. If those two fed off another human's blood, they surely would have had enough power to kill me."

"Stevie, we have to go to the police. We can talk to Dave. He's my friend and he's a good man. He'll listen."

"He's a cop. He'll see everything in black and white; he won't understand the game any better than my stepdad would."

"If you won't go to the police with me, I'll have to go alone," Regan spoke softly, gently, touching his arm as she did, "I'll have to tell them all of what Jake said last night … and I'll have to tell them about your game."

"Now that Uncle Jake's dead — what he said last night — it's your word against mine. If the police thought I had done anything wrong, they would have arrested me a long time ago.

"Last night when you had the chance, you didn't tell them everything Jake said." Stevie's eerie grin returned. "If you try to now, they won't believe you; they'll think you're a crazy lady who makes stuff up. Game over. I still win."

Regan came to the bench with one game card. She played it like a shock treatment, trying to stun him back into reality, "Jake's not dead. The call you got this morning telling you he was — it wasn't real."

Stevie greeted her news with quiescence. He took hold of her right hand, turned it palm up, and then looked into her eyes. "I didn't see your tattoo before. How could I have missed it? I thought you were on my side, but I was wrong. You're not a human, you're a minor demon."

He tucked his iPad under his arm and wiggled forward on the bench until his feet reached the ground. He dropped his voice to just above a whisper and leaned toward Regan, "If you die, Uncle Jake won't be able to feed off you," he said before he took off in the direction of the lighthouse at a brisk trot.

Stevie's menacing words pinned her to the bench. It took several seconds before she could move. When she did, she rounded the other end of the bench and sprinted toward Tom who had already started his car toward West Cliff Drive. She raced across the street to him, eliciting a beep and an unintelligible curse from a driver who had to stop quickly. She held up her hand and mouthed "Sorry" at the disgruntled driver as she opened the car door and jumped in.

"Should I follow him?" Tom queried.

"There's no time and no point. He'll go to the hospital, go

after Jake. Something happened to Stevie last night. Maybe he's finally overwhelmed with guilt, I don't know, but he's hallucinating, or dreaming at least."

Regan pulled her phone out of her purse, dialed Dave's work number, and was greeted by his efficient, "Dave Everett."

"Dave, I just talked with Stevie. I was right about him. He pretty much confessed to killing Josh Miller and Inez. I told him Jake was still alive. He may be on his way to Dominican Hospital to finish him off. Can you alert someone? Are there guards at the intensive care unit; that's where Jake is being treated, isn't it?"

"Let your little ghoul give it his best shot. He's not going to find Miller at the hospital."

"What do you mean? Where is he?"

"He's in the morgue. The info I had when I talked to you this morning was outdated. Turns out Miller died at about 4:30 this a.m. I'll alert the hospital guards that if the Butler kid turns up, they should detain him."

"Tell them he has a gun and he's delusional. Stevie said the ghosts of Jake and June Miller came to him last night, charged him with murder, and as he said, hurt him. He thinks Jakes ghost is trying to kill him."

"Humph," Dave uttered, "serves him right if Miller's ghost does haunt him. Don't worry, the hospital security guards are trained to handle crazy people. If you can say what you just told me in an affidavit, we'll get him when he turns up and hold him for a psych evaluation. That should give us enough time to put a case together and charge him with murder.

"Oh, Regan? You asked about Miller's gun arm; looks like you were right. They ran him through x-ray before surgery. His right shoulder was dislocated and not because of his gunshot wound. Must have hurt like hell especially if he tried to move his arm, but he probably couldn't."

"Stevie never took chances," she mumbled.

23

Regan was nearing the end of her speech at the annual California Association of Realtors Expo and was feeling relieved her venture into public speaking was concluding. She wasn't shy, but a packed Long Beach Convention Center room and the requirement that she speak into a microphone were intimidating. Her experience gave her a new appreciation for Dave's courage facing mic-armed local media who expected him to address thousands of viewers.

One of their own, a Santa Cruz broker who had been elected president of the association for the coming year, had heard about Regan's experience with the Murder House from Tom. He cajoled until she agreed to speak, not as a major contributor, but as a minor topic presenter in a half-day lecture about full disclosure in successful selling.

For her topic — *Selling Haunted Houses* — she used the Murder House as a specific example for how to market a stigmatized property and talked about legal disclosure requirements. She also explained how she favored a broader common sense full disclosure approach designed to keep clients and agents out of litigation. Her talk drew a larger crowd than she expected.

"As I said earlier, I'm in favor of full disclosure, especially in the case of stigmatized houses where murder, suicide, or other unnatural causes of death have occurred. Even though we in California don't have a box to check for reports of ghost sightings and paranormal activity on our disclosure forms, that doesn't mean disclosing such reported occurrences isn't a good idea, even when we don't believe such phenomena are real.

"Houses with notorious backgrounds can be sold and not necessarily at the thirty-five to fifty percent discounts some appraisers say is to be expected. You, as a real estate agent, may have to work harder or be more creative in your marketing, but you have a fiduciary responsibility to your clients which I know you take seriously. Do the necessary work. Your clients will reward you with referrals."

There was polite applause before Regan asked, "Are there any questions?"

Regan pointed to a woman with a raised hand who asked, "After your experience, are you planning to specialize in stigmatized houses?"

"No, I'm not. Perhaps if I lived on the east coast where there are many older homes with notorious histories, I might consider such a specialty niche, but where I work in Santa Cruz County, there aren't enough such properties that I could make a living."

She added a quick, "Thank goodness," and elicited a few chuckles from the audience. "And even if I could, honestly, while I learned a lot and grew my marketing skills, one haunted house was enough for me. When approached by family members to sell the Murder House after they inherited it, I declined."

Her response caused an eruption of giggles and chuckles in the room.

A broad smile lit up Regan's face. "I think they're still in the market for a competent real estate agent. Study your handouts, put together a marketing plan, and if any of you are interested, ask me for their contact information." She winked, but only those in the front row were probably aware that she had.

A young woman near the back of the room who was dressed in the most business-like suit Regan had seen in a long time stood up and announced, "I'm from the Santa Cruz area — Scotts Valley — and newly licensed. I'm struggling to get my first listing; I may take you up on that offer."

"Let's talk later," Regan suggested.

The woman sat down for the briefest of moments and then jumped to her feet again, waving to get Regan's attention as she did.

"What about the ghosts? I don't believe in ghosts," she added an "of course" as if to demonstrate her maturity and level-headedness, "but are they still around? Have there been any more sightings by neighbors?"

"Other than Stevie Butler's report of a neighbor seeing the light in the woods the night his home was visited by Jake Miller, there have been no reported sightings of the ghost in the woods since John Miller's body was exhumed and removed. The alleged ghost in the upstairs bedroom that the neighbors dubbed June Miller hasn't been seen since the murders were solved." Regan quickly added, "Some say, she's finally at peace.

"I've already rambled on longer than my allotted time. I've finished what I had to say and have been instructed to remind you that you're all invited to adjourn to the grand ballroom where there's an open bar and, I'm told, an amazing array of free appetizers for you to enjoy while you continue your networking."

Regan's heart beat faster and she clutched the mic tightly. She hadn't spoken to anyone except Tom about Stevie since his death; did she want to tell this audience what happened to him?

"But I haven't told you the rest of the story, as they say. If any of you want to give up a few minutes of your free time to remain and hear it, I'll finish my tale."

Most of the audience left, but a small group of about twenty strong stayed behind, scattered throughout the cavernous room.

"Why don't you all come closer," Regan invited. "I don't like this mic. If you move up front, you'll be able to hear me without it and we can have a real chat."

Most agents rearranged themselves into the first two rows, although a couple still held back and remained where they were. The young newbie agent from Scotts Valley had left with the crowd, but she returned in a rush carrying two glasses of red wine. She came all the way forward and handed one to Regan.

"I thought you might want this." She found one remaining seat close to Regan and sat down. "Did I miss anything?"

"Thank you ..." Regan inclined her head questioningly.

"Amber Thurston."

"Thank you, Amber. No, you didn't miss anything."

Regan had pulled a chair out of the front row and turned it to face her audience during everyone's rearranging. She sat down and leaned toward the curious to create an intimate gathering.

"We all know the rules about disclosing a death, even one by natural causes, for three years after it occurred, and we talked about the value and necessity of disclosing notorious deaths and murders which happen at properties like the Murder House, but occasionally what to do gets complicated.

"There's a continuation of the Murder House story I left out of my speech. I don't know how to disclose what happened to Stevie Butler, the young man who purchased the Murder House and killed in it, and who died there."

Regan sipped her wine before continuing.

"According to the coroner's report, Stevie died of natural causes. He had a congenital heart problem — his family was aware of it — and that's the cited cause of his death. That means only the three-year disclosure rule should apply.

"The problem is I'm not sure I completely agree with the coroner's findings. I was the last person to talk to Stevie, and at that time, he suggested another cause for his death. He spoke of being visited in the wee hours of the night by the ghost of June Miller and her lover, the newly dead Jake Miller. He said Jake's ghost tried to kill him and he expected the ghost to try again."

Many in the audience tittered nervously. Numerous legs were crossed and many arms were entwined protectively across mid-sections. But even among those who were uneasy, Regan was able to read the interested body language of her audience: they all leaned toward her, wanting more titillating details.

"At the time I dismissed what Stevie said. What I knew was that, when he told me he had been attacked the night before, though Jake Miller's grasp on life was tenuous, he was still alive, so even if I believed in ghosts, that meant Stevie's report couldn't be true."

Regan took another sip of wine and let her audience mull over what she said. "Do you all now agree that ghost sightings have no basis in fact and should never influence disclosures?"

Heads bobbed; agents agreed.

"Stevie had already tried to kill Jake Miller once; it was expected that he might go to the hospital where Jake was being treated and try again. The police were alerted and waiting for him, but Stevie never showed up to finish the job. Instead of catching Stevie in the act and arresting him, the police spent the rest of the day perfecting their charges. By the next morning, they had a warrant in hand and went to the Murder House to arrest him.

"That's when his body was discovered. He appeared, as I said, to have died of heart failure during the night."

A white-haired man in the back row spoke loudly, "I can see why you're successful. If you tell buyers to imagine what living in their new house would be like as well as you set us up with your story, I bet you sell a lot of houses."

Several people in the audience laughed in agreement.

Regan didn't. "It turns out I was mistaken about Jake Miller. He *had* died by the time Stevie thought he was attacked by ghosts. So what would you do about disclosures?

Would you follow the three-year rule, or would you add Stevie's name to the list of Murder House victims?"

Amber broke the silence that followed Regan's question.

"Oh boy, the hair on the back of my neck is standing up," her laugh was nervous. "You did say the ghosts hadn't been seen anymore, though, isn't that right? It's important for me to know, if I'm going to try to get the listing."

"I said the ghost in the woods and the female ghost hadn't been seen recently ..."

"There you go, Amber. Go for it!" the man in back shouted, interrupting Regan.

"But neighbors have reported seeing the pale ghost of a young man in the room where Stevie's body was found."

"Do you believe that stuff?" the white-haired man called out. "Have you ever seen this new ghost?"

Regan produced a smile as enigmatic as the Mona Lisa's. "We don't know one another. I think that's too personal a question for you to ask."

About the author

Nancy Lynn Jarvis finally acknowledged she's having too much fun writing to ever sell another house, so she let her license lapse in May of 2013, after her twenty-fifth anniversary in real estate.

After earning a BA in behavioral science from San Jose State University, she worked in the advertising department of the San Jose Mercury News. A move to Santa Cruz meant a new job as a librarian and later a stint as the business manager for Shakespeare/Santa Cruz at UCSC.

She invites you to take a peek into the real estate world through the stories that form the backdrop of her Regan McHenry mysteries. Real estate details and ideas come from Nancy's own experiences.

If you're one of her clients, colleagues, or contractors, read carefully — you may find characters in her books that seem familiar. You may know the person who inspired them — who knows: maybe you inspired a character yourself.

Follow Regan McHenry Real Estate Mysteries on Facebook at http://www.facebook.com/ReganMcHenryReal EstateMysteries?ref=ts

or Visit Nancy Lynn Jarvis' website http://www.GoodReadMysteries.com

where you can:

Read the first chapter of the books in the Regan McHenry Mystery Series.

Review reader comments and email your own.

Ask Nancy questions about her books and the next book in the series.

Find out about upcoming events, book club discounts, and arrange for Nancy to talk to your book club or group.

Read or print Regan's recipe for the chocolate chip cookie dough that she and Tom always have ready in their freezer.

Books are also available in large print and for your Kindle, iPad, and other e-readers.

For small presses, getting exposure in the market place dominated by big publishers is a challenge, but it is also one where you as a reader can help us enormously by spreading the word.

So, if you have enjoyed this book, please help us to promote it and other Good Read Publishers and Good Read Mysteries titles.

There's a wide range of ways you can do so, including:

- Recommending the book to your friends
- Posting a review on Amazon or other book websites
- Reviewing it on your blog
- Tweeting about it and giving a link to our website at http://www.goodreadmysteries.com
- Suggesting the book to your book club
- Posting a comment on your Facebook page
- Liking our Facebook page at http://www.facebook.com/ReganMcHenryRealEstateMysteries?ref=ts
- Pinning it at Pinterest
- Anything else that you think of!

Many thanks for your help — it's much appreciated.

The Good Read Publishers team and Nancy Lynn Jarvis

Made in the USA
San Bernardino, CA
16 January 2020